Evans Above

Evans Above

Rhys Bowen

ST. MARTIN'S PRESS ❦ NEW YORK

In writing this book I'd like to thank several people: first my grandfather for letting me borrow his name—I hope he doesn't mind—my aunt Gwladys for introducing me to the mountains of Wales and a village similar to Llanfair, Rebecca Patrascu for lending me her extensive collection of Welsh material and sharing her insights on Wales, my friends and family for their suggestions and encouragement in this new venture.

EVANS ABOVE. Copyright © 1997 by Rhys Bowen. All rights reserved. Printed in the United States of America. No part of this book may be used or reproduced in any manner whatsoever without written permission except in the case of brief quotations embodied in critical articles or reviews. For information, address St. Martin's Press, 175 Fifth Avenue, New York, N.Y. 10010.

Production Editor: David Stanford Burr

Library of Congress Cataloging-in-Publication Data

Bowen, Rhys.
    Evans above / Rhys Bowen.—1st ed.
        p.   cm.
    ISBN 0-312-16828-4
    I. Title.
PR6052.0848E93   1997
823'.914—dc21   97-24776
                                                               CIP

FIRST EDITION: DECEMBER 1997

10 9 8 7 6 5 4 3 2

Prologue

The bus groaned its way up from the coast, belching out a cloud of diesel smoke before it came to a halt outside the first house of a small village.

"Llanfair!" the driver called, looking back at the young man who sat behind him clutching a backpack.

"Is this it?" Tommy asked dubiously, peering out through the windshield at the row of slate-roofed cottages.

"This is the closest I'm going to stop," the driver said in a lilting Welsh accent. "Ask at the village. They'll tell you from there."

Tommy stepped down and hoisted his backpack onto his shoulders as the bus roared away, leaving a dark trail of smoke behind it. He stood there for a moment, taking in the unfamiliar sights and sounds—the neat rows of cottages, some whitewashed but most of them gray stone, built, Tommy suspected, with slate taken from the quarry he had noticed farther down the pass. The rows of cottages huddled under steep green slopes, down which ran parallel bright ribbons of water.

1

High above, Tommy could see white dots he knew must be sheep. Two dark specks that sped around them must be the sheepdogs, he decided. He watched, entranced, as the white dots came together into a big white blob that began moving steadily forward. Now that the bus had gone, he could hear distant baas floating down on the breeze.

It was so peaceful here—not at all as he remembered it. No sound except for the wind sighing through tall grasses and the splash and gurgle of rushing water in the stream that flowed under the humped stone bridge. Everything was so clean, as if it had been newly spring-cleaned. It smelled fresh too—a kind of green, moist scent. Tommy was glad he had decided to come after all. He needed to get away from the noise and bustle of the city, and he wanted to put some closure on this whole sad business. He was glad to know he wasn't the only one who still felt guilty about what had happened all those years ago, even though no one could be blamed. He glanced up at the distant peaks etched against a clear blue sky. How different it had been last time—the biting cold, visibility down to a few feet, the wind that took their breath away, and the freezing rain that had turned so treacherously to snow . . .

He hoisted the pack higher on his back. It would be good to see old Stew again, and maybe Jimmy as well. He presumed one of them must have sent the postcard . . . it had to be one of Danny's close friends in their little gang from hut 29.

He was about to cross the bridge when he noticed that someone was perched on the parapet in the shade of a mountain ash tree, sitting still as a statue. As he came closer he saw the mailman's uniform and was amused to note that the mailman was engrossed in reading the mail.

"Excuse me," he said. "Am I going the right way for the Everest Inn?"

2

The mailman looked up and stared at him vacantly as if he was a visitor from Mars.

"Everest Inn?" Tommy asked again, wondering if the man could speak English.

The man hastily gathered the letters, shoving them into his bag, before he took off in the other direction with long loping strides.

Tommy shrugged and started up the village street. Not a soul was about. Even the pub seemed to be closed. Of course, they probably still observed strict drinking laws in this godforsaken corner of Wales. He remembered how unfriendly they'd been before, looking up with wary eyes and switching to Welsh the moment he and his mates had walked into the bar.

Across the street was a little row of shops. G. Evans, Butcher, stood next to R. Evans, Dairy Products. Only T. Harris, General Store, spoiled the Evans monopoly. He could see someone moving behind the counter in the butcher shop, so he pushed open the door and went in.

"Bore da." A large florid man wearing a soiled apron greeted him in Welsh.

"Hello," Tommy said in his cheerful cockney. "Nice day, isn't it? I'm looking for the Everest Inn."

The man's face became instantly remote. "Everest Inn, is it?"

"Yeah, they told me it was around here."

"You can't miss it," the butcher said, then muttered under his breath, "Bloody great monstrosity!"

"What's the matter with it?"

"Nobody wanted it built here, did they? Brings a lot of foreigners and too much traffic."

Tommy smiled. He hadn't seen a single car go past since he got off the bus. The man had gone back to chopping up a lamb carcass on the marble slab, swinging a murderous-looking cleaver down with rhythmic strokes.

"So how do I find it?" Tommy asked cautiously.

The man didn't look up and continued chopping. "Keep going through the village, past the chapels, and up the hill. You can't miss it."

"Thanks. Cheers," Tommy said, and half raised his hand in a friendly wave. As he came out of the door into the warm, spring sunshine, a milk van had just drawn up and a tall, skinny man in a milkman's cap was coming up the steps. He gave Tommy a little half nod, then called out something in Welsh to the butcher and laughed loudly. Tommy turned back in time to see the butcher wave the cleaver at him with a threatening gesture, yelling after him what sounded like a torrent of Welsh insults. The words echoed from the narrow valley walls.

"Go boil your head, Evans-the-Meat," the milkman called, still laughing. "I was only joking. You take everything too seriously."

"Is that a fact? Well, I don't find your jokes very funny, Evans-the-Milk," the butcher yelled back. "And don't think you can insult me. You come from a very inferior branch of the family."

"Inferior, is it? To whom, I'd like to know!"

"Can *you* trace *your* ancestry back to the Great Llewellyn himself? Related to that dafty at the post office, that's what you are."

The rest of the argument was lost as Tommy walked on up the street. Personally, he wouldn't have risked trading insults with a man who had chopped through a lamb carcass as if he was cutting butter.

The street was still deserted. The sign outside the Red

Dragon pub swung gently in the wind. As he passed the school he heard the sound of young voices and saw twenty or so little kids in uniform skipping in a circle around a slim young woman. She wore a long skirt, a white blouse, and embroidered ethnic vest. A single braid of corn-colored hair hung way down her back, and she looked as if she had stepped straight out of an Arthurian romance. Tommy paused to watch her as she clapped the rhythm and the children skipped and sang. He tried to pick up the words of the chant, but realized that they were singing in Welsh. That was the trouble with Wales—you didn't think it was a foreign country, but it was.

The pack was weighing heavily on his shoulders and the wind was now blowing briskly from the pass as he climbed up the street. As the road swung around, he could see the imposing shape of the inn interrupting the green sweep of hills at the head of the pass. As he came closer, he could see that it was built like an overgrown Swiss chalet, complete with gingerbread trim and geranium-decked balconies. No wonder the locals hadn't welcomed it—it *was* a bloody great monstrosity.

The last two buildings in the village were both Methodist chapels, as was usual in this part of the world. They were identical gray slate buildings with modest spires and notice boards outside. One announced Chapel Bethel, Sunday School 10 A.M., Worship Service 6 P.M. (Sermon in English). The other said, in Welsh, with a small English translation below it, Chapel Beulah, Sunday Worship 10 A.M. and 6 P.M. Sermon in English and Welsh.

Under these notices were billboards, each containing a text. The text outside Bethel read, "Keep watchful for ye know not when the end shall come." Tommy was amused to see that the text outside Beulah read, "Judgement Day is tomorrow."

Tommy chuckled all the way up the hill until the chill wind blowing from the heights made him suddenly shiver. He paused and glanced back down the valley. He wondered if he was doing the right thing coming here after all . . .

High above, the mountain watched and waited.

Chapter 1

The sound of singing rose up from the little village of Llanfair, nestled high on the pass between the great peaks of Glyder Fawr and Yr Wyddfa. On the green slopes above, sheep looked up, momentarily startled by the burst of sound, then went back to their grazing, their wool tinged pink by the setting sun.

Guide me, oh Thou great Jehova
Pilgrim in this barren land . . .

The words of that favorite old Welsh hymn, *Cwm Rhonda*, resounded around Chapel Bethel as only Welsh voices can sing it. If Chapel Bethel had rafters instead of polystyrene tiles, the hymn would have definitely have made them ring.

Only one person was not joining in lustily. A tall young man with the broad shoulders of a rugby forward and a fresh, likeable face, was only mouthing the words.

I am weak, but Thou art mighty
Feed me with Thy willing hand.

Evan Evans was a constable with the North Wales police force, currently assigned to the village of Llanfair. He could feel the familiar flush rising at the back of his neck and spreading over his fair-skinned Celtic face. He knew it was stupid to be troubled by something that had happened so many years ago, but he couldn't help it. Every time they sang that particular hymn in chapel he was back in the assembly hall at Llanelli Road County Primary School, standing in the front row of top class boys and hearing the giggles behind him as two hundred young voices sang the chorus.

Bread of 'eaven
Bread of 'eaven
Feed me till I want no more . . .

Sang the worshippers in Chapel Bethel now. P.C. Evans could almost feel the digs in his back and hear the giggles and whispered comments: "What kind of bread have you got for us today then, Evan boy? Crusty, is it?"

He had only just arrived at the Llanelli Road school, a skinny, undersized kid of ten, fresh from the mountains of North Wales and no match for the tough dockland boys at his new school. Every time they sang that hymn Evan Evans cursed his parents for giving him such a stupid name. Now he was a grown man, liked and respected, and pretty handy with his fists too when needed, but that hymn still had the power to make him feel uncomfortable.

He could almost hear the taunts now. He was sure of it.

Someone was whispering behind him. Any second now, someone was going to dig him in the back and whisper, "What kind of bread then, Evan bach?"

At last the desire to turn around proved too strong. He glanced back and saw two men standing by the side entrance. One of them was old Charlie Hopkins, the usher, and he was pointing directly at Evan. The other man looked familiar, but Even couldn't place him right away. He was middle-aged but fit-looking. His face was tanned but his age was betrayed by hair graying at the sides and combed across to hide a bald spot. He was dressed in a large polo-necked Nordic sweater and cords. As Evan stared at him in surprise, Charlie Hopkins beckoned furiously for him to come over.

Evan glanced around then tiptoed toward the door. Charlie Hopkins grabbed his arm and whispered in his ear, "They've been and gone and done it again, Constable Evans."

Evan stepped out into the summer twilight. Here, between tall peaks, the sun set early. "Done what?" he asked, looking for help to the stranger who stood beside Mr. Hopkins.

"One of they climbers, that's what," Mr. Hopkins said. "Got himself stuck on Yr Wyddfa again." He called the mountain that the English knew as Snowdon by its Welsh name, even though he addressed Evan in English because of the stranger.

"Not again!" Evan said, raising his eyes in despair. "How many weeks has it been since we had a Sunday without a rescue call, eh, Charlie? What's happened this time?" He looked inquiringly at the stranger, trying to place him.

"This is Constable Evans, major," Charlie said. "He leads our little rescue squad. He's quite an expert climber."

"Really?" The man couldn't have sounded less impressed.

"You know Major Anderson, don't you, Evan boy?" Charlie said. "He's the manager at the Everest Inn up the valley. You know the place I'm talking about, don't you?"

Evan gave the major a friendly grin. "It would be hard not to know it, wouldn't it? Takes up half the valley, doesn't it?" Privately he thought it was one of the ugliest buildings he had ever seen. He had never understood the reasoning behind building a Swiss chalet in the middle of Wales. It had opened only the season before, just after Evan himself had arrived in Llanfair, and its guests had kept the village mountain rescue team busy ever since.

But Evan kept his thoughts to himself. He thrust out a big hand. "How do, Major Anderson. Yes, we have met before. Got a climber in trouble again, have you, major? Why don't you teach those climbers of yours how to climb before you let them loose on the mountains?" He had meant it as a good-natured tease, but he saw the smile fade from the major's face.

"Rather worrying, what?" Major Anderson said in a throaty, upper-class English voice. "These chappies always say they know how to climb. Set off with all the right equipment and they always underestimate our Welsh mountains. Think they're not like the Alps or Himalayas, eh, what?"

Evan managed to keep the annoyance from his face. He remembered his last encounter with the major clearly now. He'd been called in to investigate the theft of a diamond and the major had been obnoxiously patronizing, calling him "My dear chappy" and implying that a mere village constable wasn't up to the job. Like most people in Wales, Evan didn't have much time for people who went around giving themselves airs and calling themselves major when they weren't in the army any more . . . or who referred to the mountains as "our Welsh mountains" when he probably hadn't a drop of Welsh blood in him.

Evan gave the major a congenial smile. "Funny, isn't it? There must be a lot of people who can't tell our mountains from the Alps. The people who built your inn, for example. It's a wonder they don't have you wearing short leather trousers and showing your knees."

"Ah, quite. Yes. Ha-ha. Most amusing," the major said.

Evan remembered with some satisfaction that the major had called again, later that same night, to say that the guest had found her missing diamond, hidden in the toe of her fuzzy slippers, where she had put it for safekeeping. He hadn't apologized.

Evan put on his most efficient manner as he turned to the major. "So you've had a message that one of your climbers is in trouble?" Evan asked. "Got himself stuck on Crib Goch, has he?"

"No message," Major Anderson said. "Just hasn't come back down, that's all. Set off after breakfast this morning and nobody's seen him since."

Evan looked up at the dark outline of the Snowdon range, silhouetted against a silver sky dotted with pink clouds. Wisps of cloud clung in the gullies like sheep wool caught on a fence.

"It's not even dark yet," he said. "Give him time. He was probably enjoying the sunset. Beautiful day, wasn't it? I was up there myself, earlier today. Did you know there's a red kite's nest with babies in it? That's good news, isn't it? Haven't seen one of them for years."

"Er, quite." Major Anderson cut him off. "But to get back to the point, constable. I wouldn't have come to you if I wasn't concerned."

"He was definitely planning to come back to you tonight, was he then?"

"Oh yes, definitely," Major Anderson said. "He told the staff he'd be in for dinner."

"And you think he was planning to go climbing, not just walking?"

Major Anderson sucked his teeth as he thought. "I couldn't actually say," he admitted. "He asked for the easiest way up Snowdon and said he was meeting a friend up there. But he was wearing pretty decent boots and he did have a pack. So maybe he was planning to do some climbing with his friend, once he was up there."

"There you are then," Evan said. "He met the friend and they decided to go down another way together. Probably went down on the railway to Llanberis. Like as not they're having a drink there now and the friend will run him back here later in his car."

"But he said he'd dine here," Major Anderson said patiently, as if Evan was a slow two-year-old. "And he knows that dinner is at seven o'clock sharp. He'd need time to change, wouldn't he? We have a very strict dress code in the dining room."

"Maybe he's changed his mind," Evan suggested. "People are allowed to change their minds, you know." He turned to wink at Charlie. "It's not the army, is it?"

A spasm of a frown crossed the major's face. "Obviously you don't share my concern, constable. I have my hotel to think of. People stranded on the mountain are bad publicity for us. Rescues always seem to make the TV news, don't they? If he's stuck up there, I want him brought down right away."

"Hold on a minute," Evan said, putting a calming hand on the major's shoulder. "If the gentleman was going up the Pig Track or the Miners' Track, straight to the top of Snowdon, he'd have been on a well-travelled route. If he'd hurt himself, or got himself into trouble, we'd have heard about it. There's nowhere on that route that he could have got himself stuck, is there? Like a bloody great motorway, isn't it? And just as well travelled."

He found himself thinking back to his early childhood spent among these mountains and to the happy days with his grandfather up in the high country. In those days it seemed that it was just the two of them, alone on the roof of the world, sometimes in the clouds, sometimes above them, with eagles soaring below their feet.

But now it was hard to find a place of solitude, even for someone like Evan who knew these mountains like the back of his hand. Most frequently he'd be settled and sunk into contemplation when laughter and loud voices on the path below would announce the arrival of another group of tourists. They'd stagger up the path, often clad in the most unsuitable clothes—shorts and T-shirts—no foul weather gear in case the cloud came in, sandals or city shoes, videotaping as they went. It was all a big lark to them. They had no idea that a storm could roll in and blow them off the path with gale force winds, or that the cloud could come down and blot out the way back, that one step off the path could lead to destruction, and that a night on the mountains could finish them off.

"Give him until morning, major," he said, drawing his mind back to the present problem. "I can't have my lads missing their chapel over every climber who comes back late, can I? Likely as not you'll have heard from him by morning. I'd wager your boy shows up late for dinner, or gives you a ring from Llanberis. And if he is stranded up there for the night . . . well, it's not going to be too cold, is it and he could always make for the kiosk and shelter there. It might teach him a lesson about taking our Welsh mountains more seriously."

He smiled at the major. "Now, if you'll excuse me, I have to get back to chapel. I don't want to miss the reverend Parry Davies' sermon. Heard about him, have you? He's a famous orator. Goes to the eisteddfods every year and wins prizes, and gives powerful good sermons—all hellfire and damnation. You can almost smell the brimstone. The Reverend Powell-Jones has had to have double glazing put on his windows."

His gaze drifted across the street to the other chapel, Beulah, where the Reverend Powell-Jones was conducting his own evening worship. He made up for his lack of Parry Davies' power of oratory by giving his sermons in Welsh and then in English. Since this took well over an hour, his congregation was considerably smaller than Bethel's—mainly old women who had grown up as Welsh speakers and ardent nationalists. Still, it was hard to compete against Bethel's added advantage: A footpath behind it that led to the back door of the Red Dragon.

Even though all the pubs in Wales were now officially allowed to open on Sundays, Llanfair was one of those pockets of religious righteousness where Sunday drinking was still outwardly frowned upon, and the front door of the pub remained firmly shut to strangers. The back door, however, was open to admit regular customers, which was why most of the men of Llanfair attended evening services at Chapel Bethel.

"Do I understand that you're refusing to do anything to help?" the major blustered. "I'm going to have a word with your superiors about this."

"When I get word that someone's in trouble, then I'll be all too willing to help, major," Evan said. "So will all the lads in the village. But we're all volunteers, you know. We can't go wandering all over the mountains looking for someone who might not even be up there by now. It's going to be dark soon

14

and I can't risk losing one of my lads over a cliff, can I? Look, why don't you call me in the morning if he hasn't shown up. But right now God and Mr. Parry Davies are calling, if you don't mind."

The major strode off, muttering, "Oh, this is absurd. Completely useless. Village idiots, the lot of them . . ."

Charlie Hopkins turned back to Evan with an apologetic shrug. "You don't suppose we should have gone, do you, Evan bach? That's the type who likes to make trouble. Got friends in high places."

Evan scowled at the major's disappearing back. "If he had friends in the right sort of high places," he said pointing up at the silhouette of the mountain, "then they could bloody well look for his missing climber themselves and leave us in peace."

Charlie Hopkins chuckled and reluctantly Evan laughed, too. "I'm sorry, Charlie, but that man gets my goat. Barkin' orders as if he was still in the army. We're only volunteers, after all. Nobody pays us to go traipsing over mountains, ruining our good shoes and missing our chapel."

Mr. Hopkins dug Evan in the side. "Don't let me keep you then, constable," he said. "You'll be wanting to get back for the rest of the sermon, I don't doubt."

He winked at Evan.

"After you, Mr. Hopkins," Evan said, giving him a little shove in the direction of the chapel door. "You're the usher. You have to be there to collect the hymn books, don't you?"

Mr. Hopkins looked at the chapel door and then let his gaze wander further down the street to where the Red Dragon pub sign was swinging in the evening breeze. "They all know where the hymn books go," he said. "And it sounds like the Reverend Parry Davies is cutting it short tonight. He must be as thirsty as we are. No sense in going back in there just for one

15

last hymn, is there? Might as well get our orders in first next door." He nudged Evan again. "Give you a chance to be alone in the pub for a while with you know who."

His lean body shook with silent laughter.

Evan sighed. Ever since he had come here a year ago, the entire valley had tried its best to play matchmaker. Betsy, the barmaid in the Red Dragon, had made no secret of the fact that she fancied Evan.

"Get away with you now, Charlie," Evan said, flushing with embarrassment. "Betsy's a nice girl and all that but not exactly my type, you know."

"You could do worse, Evan boy." Charlie chuckled. "I hear she's ready, willing, and very able."

"That's the trouble, Charlie," Evan said with a grin. "She's too ready and too willing. If I so much as say hello to her, she takes it as encouragement. She's always on about taking her dancing in Caernarfon."

"And what's wrong with that?" Charlie asked.

Evan shook her head. "You've never seen me dance," he said. "They tell me I look like a dying octopus. Besides, I'm not ready to get involved with anybody yet. Only just got here, haven't I?"

He had his back to the street and hadn't heard anyone coming, so he jumped when a soft voice said, "Good evening, Constable Evans. Not in chapel tonight, I see?"

Evan spun around to see a slim young woman smiling at him. She was dressed in khaki pants and a linen shirt. A dark green sweater was draped around her neck and brought out the green in her eyes. Her hair hung down her back in one lustrous braid. As always Evan felt tongue-tied in her presence.

"Good evening, Bronwen Price," Evan stammered. "I see you're not in chapel yourself either."

16

Bronwen took in Evan's jacket and tie. He must have been intending to go to chapel anyway, she thought. He wasn't the kind of person who wore a jacket when he didn't have to. Usually he was the old-jeans-and-sweater type. Out of uniform he looked quite handsome, she thought. She liked the way his dark hair flopped down boyishly across his forehead when he wasn't wearing his policeman's cap.

"I've just got back from an all-day hike," she said. "Did you know that a red kite is nesting up there now? Isn't that wonderful news?"

"Up above Llyn Llydaw? I saw it myself," Evan said, his face lighting up.

"You did?" Bronwen looked surprised. "When were you up there?"

"Earlier today."

"You were? Pity we missed each other."

"Great pity," Evan said with feeling. Then, suddenly awkward again with Charlie Hopkins looking on, he stammered, "Two babies in the nest, wasn't it?"

Charlie looked from Evan to Bronwen. "I'll just nip on ahead to the Red Dragon then," he said. "Let them know you're coming."

Evan looked at Bronwen. "You feel like a drink?"

"On a Sunday?" At first Evan thought that Bronwen sounded genuinely shocked, but then he noticed that her eyes were teasing. "What would my pupils say if they saw their teacher going into the pub on a Sunday night?"

"I thought it might be thirsty work, all that hiking," Evan said.

"You're right, it was," Bronwen agreed with a smile.

"Then the drink is for medicinal purposes," Evan said. "It's a known fact that you have to replenish fluids after strenuous exercise—and we'll go the back way by the footpath. Nobody will see you."

Bronwen laughed. "There's nothing they don't see or know in this village, but I'll come along to keep you company, if you like. Not that I approve of playing hookey from chapel."

"I'll have you know I was called out on official business," Evan said. "Another lost climber." He stood aside to let Bronwen go ahead of him as they started down the little footpath.

"Not again," Bronwen said over her shoulder. "They should make them pass a test before they let them loose on the mountain."

"Now that would be a good idea," Evan said.

"I see you aren't in a hurry to go and find him," Bronwen said.

"If I went to find every climber who was half an hour late for dinner, I might as well forget my day job and live in a tent up on the mountain," Evan said. "We'll hear about it soon enough if he's really in trouble. It's not even dark yet."

He paused outside the pub and looked appreciatively at the dark outlines of the mountains, etched against a pure rose pink sky. "Going to be a beautiful day again tomorrow," he said, as he shepherded Bronwen into the back door of the Red Dragon.

Chapter 2

Up on the mountain the sun sank, plunging the cliffs into deep shadow so that it was hard to discern what it was that lay among the rocks. A chill wind sprang up, howling through the crevices and drowning a cry that nobody heard.

Betsy, the barmaid, looked up expectantly as Charlie Hopkins came into the pub.

"Good evening, Mr. Hopkins," she said. "Don't tell me you're the only one drinking tonight?"

Charlie glanced back at the door. "Chapel's not out yet, Betsy bach. Constable Evans and I were called out on an emergency so we got a head start."

"Constable Evans isn't coming then?" she asked, the disappointment showing in her wide blue eyes.

"He's coming right enough," Charlie said, "But he's taking his time about it. He got waylaid." His eyes danced with wicked merriment.

"You mean he's with someone?" Betsy demanded. "Not that Bronwen Price?"

"My lips are sealed," Charlie said. "Give me a pint of best bitter, will you love?"

Betsy pulled the pint as if she was wringing a chicken's neck. "Bronwen Bloody Price. Don't tell me he sees anything in her." she demanded. "What is there to see under all those clothes she wears? Most men like a woman to look like a woman, don't they, Charlie?"

She pulled down the low-necked angora sweater she was wearing to emphasize the point.

Charlie didn't like to say that Bronwen wasn't wearing her usual voluminous skirts tonight and that she looked very neat and trim in her hiking gear.

"No doubt he's only being friendly, isn't it?" Betsy said to reassure herself as she put the overflowing glass in front of Charlie Hopkins. "He's a very friendly person, wouldn't you say, Mr. Hopkins?"

"Very friendly," Charlie said. He was thinking that Evan and Bronwen were taking an awful long time to walk a few yards.

Betsy's eyes widened as the door opened and Evan's voice could be heard. She smoothed down her sweater again. Just let that Bronwen Price try her best—a poor specimen of woman-hood she was. No curves to speak of and no makeup either. What had she got to offer a man on cold winter's nights?

Betsy watched Evan come in and lead Bronwen through to the lounge on the other side of the bar. Even though there was no written rule, it was generally accepted that women didn't belong in the public bar with the men. It was a brave woman who defied this tradition. Betsy watched with annoyance as

20

Evan pulled out a chair for Bronwen, who smiled at him as she sat down. He took off his jacket and hung it over the back of his chair. Betsy's eyes lingered appreciatively on his broad back. She liked them well built. She imagined herself unbuttoning that white shirt some day and running her hands over those big shoulders. She lowered her eyes and pretended to be busy as he headed for the bar.

"Evening, Betsy," he said. "I'd like a pint of Guinness for myself, and . . ." He lowered his voice, glancing around to see if anyone was in earshot. "A Perrier for the lady."

"A Perrier?" Betsy's nose wrinkled and she glanced across at Bronwen. She went to the fridge and carried the bottle back between two fingers. "Waste of money, if you ask me," she said. "Might as well go and take a drink from the stream."

Evan tried not to smile. He knew from experience that she took every smile as encouragement and he certainly didn't want to encourage her in front of Bronwen.

"And Guinness for you, is it, Evan bach?" she asked, pouring the pint glass so full that it slopped over. "I like a man with a good healthy appetite," she added, running her tongue over her full lips. Even felt himself flushing.

"Thanks, Betsy," he said, fishing for money in his pocket. He put the money on the bar.

"If you're free later," she said in a low voice as he picked up the glasses, "I've rented this very interesting video from the store in Caernarfon. It's Italian—all about the dolce vita in Rome. I can't understand a word of what they're saying, but you don't really need to, do you?"

Evan tried to think of something to say, but his mind was a blank. He was trying hard to keep his eyes from straying to Betsy's cleavage. She was pressing herself up against the bar as she spoke, which pulled her neckline even lower, and he knew she was doing it quite deliberately. He found himself wondering, just for a moment, what it would be like if . . .

"So, do you feel like coming over later?" she asked again. "I always get out early on Sundays, seeing as how it's only the regulars."

"Can't tonight, love," he said. "We had a missing climber call. I'd have to stay by the phone, wouldn't I?"

With that he hurried the beer and the Perrier to the table, before Betsy could come up with any more interesting suggestions.

"Sorry," he said, putting the Perrier in front of Bronwen.

"That's all right," Bronwen said politely, "I could see you were—otherwise occupied." Her eyes strayed across to the bar. "She tries hard, doesn't she?" she went on. "I'd have to give her an A for effort."

"She means well," Evan said charitably.

"I'm sure she does," Bronwen said.

"She never takes no for an answer, that's the problem," Evan said. "And I don't like to be rude . . ."

"Of course not," Bronwen said smoothly.

Evan had just sat down opposite Bronwen when the chapel crowd came in, talking noisily.

"What was that all about then, Constable Evans?" one of the men demanded. "Was that the major I saw call you out of chapel?"

"Indeed it was, Mr. Rees. One of his climbers was late for dinner and he wanted us to go find him."

"The man's got a nerve," someone else growled. "Anyone would think we did this for a living."

"So what did you tell him, Evan bach? I hope you told him where to get off?"

22

"I can tell you what I'd like to have told him, but there are ladies present," Evan said, getting a chuckle all around. "He got quite put out when I said I wasn't calling you lads out tonight and wandering all over the mountains looking for his climber."

"Quite right, Evan bach," one of the men agreed. "Nothing but trouble that Everest Inn has been since it was built."

Evan turned to smile at Bronwen as the men crowded around the bar.

"I get the feeling that the major isn't your favorite person," she said.

"You can say that again," Evan said. "That man gets my goat, Bronwen. He reminds me of my old headmaster at school—he had the same accent and he was always looking down at me because I was only a scholarship boy."

Bronwen looked up with interest. "A scholarship boy? Where?"

"Down in Swansea. Swansea Grammar School—do you know it?" Evan asked. "Very posh. My parents were so proud when I got a scholarship there."

"I thought everyone said you were from around here."

"I was born up here. We moved to Swansea when I was a little kiddy. My dad got a job down there, see, so we had to move."

"That must have been hard for you, moving to the big city."

"It was pretty tough. And then I got a scholarship to this posh school and that was even harder. They used to make fun of me because my English wasn't too good in those days and because I was undersized and skinny."

Bronwen laughed. "You? Undersized and skinny? You certainly changed."

Evan smiled too. "They changed their tune at school when I started growing and turned into a useful rugby player. By the time I left, I was twice the size of that headmaster and he couldn't look down his nose at me any more, even if he'd wanted to."

"What made your father move down to Swansea?" Bronwen asked. "Did he work in the docks?"

"He was a copper," Evan said. "They paid more down there."

"So you're following in your father's footsteps then?"

Evan's face grew solemn. "Something like that," he said.

"And what made you come back up here?"

He paused. "I'd had enough of Swansea," he said quickly. "What about you? What made you come here?"

She shrugged. "I wanted the simple life," she said. "Back to basics. I wanted to teach kids who still had a sense of innocence and wonder. No drugs or gangs or shopping centers."

"Do you really believe that we can shut out the world in a place like this?" he asked quietly.

"I hope so," she said.

Evan looked down at his hands. "Sometimes I wonder."

The door opened again, sending in a blast of cold air that swirled napkins on tables.

"If it isn't Evans-the-Meat," the milkman said loudly. "So the service at that other chapel finally got out, did it? Where are the others, or have they all fallen asleep in their pews?"

Evans-the-Meat stared at him coldly. "Just because our minister is a good Welshman who chooses to give his sermon in his native tongue, there's no need to mock it. If only there were more patriotic men here who cared more for their native tongue and less for their beer."

Evans-the-Milk stepped forward to meet him. "Are you

24

saying I'm less patriotic than you? Who forgot to wear the leek last St. David's day, huh?"

"Was it my fault that my wife forgot what day it was and put my leek in her mutton stew?" Evans-the-Meat demanded, the color rising so that his face looked like a large, round beetroot. "My side of the family can be traced back to Llewellyn the Great and that's about as patriotic as you can get."

"Are you trying to say I'm not as Welsh as you are?"

Evan noticed the clenched fists and got ready to intervene. It wouldn't be the first time that the two men had come to blows in the pub. He had just begun to get to his feet when the door opened again. A young boy burst in, cheeks bright red from the wind and out of breath from running.

"Is Evans-the-Law here?" he gasped, looking around at the men at the bar. "Tell him he's wanted on the mountain. They've found a body."

Chapter 3

The next morning Evan stood beside Detective Sergeant Watkins, summoned from North Wales police in Caernarfon. They had located the body the night before, but given the difficult nature of the terrain, it had been too dangerous to do anything more until first light. The wind whipped at their clothing as they stood together on a narrow ledge, looking down at the body that lay sprawled far below. Even from this high vantage point, they could see the dark stain on the granite where the man lay.

"Nasty accident," Sergeant Watkins said, sucking through his teeth, "but I can't see why you called us in, Constable Evans. We're busy down at headquarters right now. We haven't got time to check out climbing accidents."

Evan took his eyes from the horrifying sight of the sprawled body and glanced at the detective. He was a small, lean man, thirtyish, with a colorless, humorless face, made more colorless by light red hair and a fawn raincoat.

"You think it was an accident then, do you?" Evan asked.

27

Sergeant Watkins looked up sharply. "Of course. What else could it be? An inexperienced climber loses his footing or his nerve on the ledge, gets vertigo, and tumbles over."

"Begging your pardon, sarge, but not even a bloody Englishman could fall off the ledge right here," Evan said. "By afternoon the wind's rushing up from the lowlands so strong that you could almost lie in it. And see how the rock angles backward? If you lost your footing or your nerve here, you'd fall back into the rock face, not down the cliff."

"So what are you saying, constable?"

"I'm saying that someone had to have helped him get where he is now."

"Pushed him, you mean? You're trying to tell me this was deliberate?"

Evan shrugged. "Maybe it was accidental, sarge. Maybe he was with a companion who slipped and accidentally pushed him over, then was too scared to come forward and confess. That happens too, you know. But if you did want to get rid of somebody, this wouldn't be a bad way to do it."

Sergeant Watkins looked at Evan speculatively, then shook his head in disbelief.

"Come on now, constable," he said. "How many people do you think there were up on the mountain yesterday? Somebody would have seen or heard . . ."

"It would only take a second. One quick shove when he wasn't looking," Evan said.

Sergeant Watkins shook his head again. "You've been reading too many crime novels," he said. Then his tone softened. "Look, I can understand. It must be boring stuck out in a little village with only old ladies and their missing pussycats to keep you occupied. A nice juicy murder would spice things up, wouldn't it?" He paused and cleared his throat. "Down at HQ we've got a real murder on our hands. Someone dumped an eleven-year-old girl's body in a ditch beside the A55. She'd been strangled and sexually assaulted. A little eleven-year-old! I want to find the bastard that did that, Constable Evans. It's all I can think about right now. So I don't think I've got time to waste on a climber who lost his footing and fell over a cliff."

"Maybe we'll know more when we find out who he is, sarge," Evan said. "If he's a missing heir or police informant, then will you believe me?"

The detective managed a smile. "Very well, constable. Maybe we'll know more when we can get the body out, but I doubt it. You're not going to find a handprint in the middle of his back."

"Someone might have seen something," Evan said. "You could ask people to come forward if they saw anything suspicious."

Sergeant Watkins looked at him. "I can tell you're dying to get yourself involved in a murder, constable, but you're wasting your time. I've got my photographer coming to take pictures, then we'll have to decide the best way to get him out."

Evan let his gaze move down to the body, which was lodged among jagged rocks at the base of the cliff. Below it the ground fell away again and ended in a murderously steep slope of scree that met the western shore of the mountain lake Glaslyn.

"And that's not going to be easy," Sergeant Watkins added. "I might have to call down to HQ and see if the chief can spare us the helicopter."

"My lads can probably do it," Evan said.

"Your lads?"

"We have a local mountain rescue squad in our village. All the men there grew up when the slate quarries were still working. They're used to walking up and down cliffs. Born to it, they are around here. They walk up and down these mountains like they're crossing an open field—and in their best Sunday polished shoes if there's a real necessity for it."

"Is that so," Sergeant Watkins said, fishing in his pocket for his notebook.

There was the scrunch of boots farther along the ledge and a young policeman came toward them, jauntily swinging a camera.

"Hello, sarge. I got the pictures you wanted."

What do you mean, you got them?" Sergeant Watkins asked sharply. "Where did you get them from?"

"Over above Llyn Llydaw where you're looking down on the body. Isn't that what you wanted?"

"Above Llyn Llydaw? What are you talking about? The body's right here."

The young policeman peered down over the edge. "Christ," he exclaimed. "Then there are two of them!"

It took fifteen minutes to pick their way back up to the main trail and then around the lip of the mountain until they were overlooking Llyn Llydaw, the lower of the two Snowdon lakes. From the summit of Snowdon, the mountains extended in a horseshoe, almost encircling the two lakes, but a spur jutted out at one point, separating Glaslyn, the higher of the two, from the lower lake. The ridge was knife-edged all the way around and the cliffs ringing the lakes were unrelentingly sheer.

"Down there," the police photographer said. "He must have fallen over the edge of the ridge, don't you think? It's steep enough around here and the wind gusts are nasty too. It nearly knocked my camera out of my hands when I was trying to get the pictures. I hope you don't want me to get down to him—I never did have a good head for heights."

Again the man was lying face down at the bottom of a cliff, his arms sprawled outward as if he had tried desperately to break his fall.

"It's a wonder nobody reported seeing this happen," the young photographer went on. "It was a fine day yesterday, wasn't it? The mountain must have been swarming with hikers and tourists."

"This isn't on any of the main routes up the mountain," Evan said, gazing down. If either of these men was the climber missing from the Everest Inn, then they hadn't taken the quickest way up to the summit. "The only real path is the one we've been taking along the ridge," he said. "It goes over the top of Lliwedd before it drops down to the valley."

"Maybe he'd been to the top and was attempting a short-cut down," the photographer suggested.

"A shortcut, down here?" Sergeant Watkins eyed the sheer granite below. "He'd have been bloody stupid, unless he was trying to do some climbing."

Evan shook his head. "He wasn't a climber. Look at his feet. He's wearing ordinary running shoes. He'd never have tried climbing in those. He probably came up on the train. And he doesn't have any rope with him."

"Maybe he got it into his head to try his hand at it, even though he didn't have the equipment," Sergeant Watkins suggested. "People are always doing daft things, aren't they? They see it on the telly and it looks easy enough. He was trying to climb up this cliff, lost his grip, and fell."

Evan shook his head. "He fell forwards, sarge. If he'd been climbing up he'd have landed on his back."

"It was bad luck, whatever it was," Sergeant Watkins said. He was already starting to turn away. "Got enough pictures,

31

Dawson? Good, then let's get back and radio HQ to have them brought out."

Evan fell into step with him. "You still think it was a coincidence, sarge?" he asked. "Two men falling off the mountain in one afternoon?"

Detective Sergeant Watkins was staring straight ahead. "Yes, I think it was a couple of unlucky accidents, Constable Evans," he said. "If it wasn't, what's the alternative? You think we've got a madman running around pushing people off the mountain?"

Young Constable Dawson squeezed in between them. "You think it could have been deliberate then?"

"Constable Evans does," Sergeant Watkins said, "but then he leads a lonely life with all these sheep up here. He's just itching for a touch of excitement."

"Not really, sarge," Evan said calmly. "I saw plenty of excitement when I was in detective training, down in Swansea. We had a murder a night sometimes, down in dockland."

"You were in detective training down in Swansea?" Constable Dawson asked with envy in his voice. "So what on earth made you give that up to come here?"

"You can have too much of a good thing," Evan said. "Let's just say I'd seen one murder too many."

"I can understand that," Sergeant Watkins said. "That little kiddy we've got now. I don't think I'll ever forget how she looked when we found her in that ditch. I'll never be able to get that little face out of my mind as long as I live. Looked as if she was asleep at first—just like our little Tiffany when I check on her."

His voice cracked and he put his hand to his mouth and coughed as if embarrassed about showing such emotion. Evan began to feel more kindly toward him.

"Got any leads yet, sarge?" he asked.

"One that looks promising. We've found out that a convicted child molester called Lou Walters was released from Pentonville Prison early and has a mother who lives in Caernarfon. Have you heard about this latest stunt they've pulled on us? They've been quietly letting prisoners out of jail early to avoid overcrowding and not telling anyone. The Home Secretary is livid. Heads are going to roll, mark my words, but it's too late to lock the stable when the horse has already bolted, isn't it?"

"Have you managed to track this child molester?" Evan asked.

"No, but we've got a watch on his mother's house. He'll show up there sooner or later. We'll be sending out a description of him to all the substations for you to keep your eyes open."

"I hope you get him before he gets his hands on any more kiddies," Evan said.

"Me too," Sergeant Watkins said.

"And what are we going to do about these two?" Evan asked.

Sergeant Watkins looked back. "Get them out and notify their next of kin. That's all we can do, isn't it?"

"Better hurry up about it then, before the weather changes," Evan said. He glanced out across the foothills to the ocean. The sun was still shining but the horizon was now a hard line. That meant rain before too long.

"I'd imagine our men could get them into a position where a helicopter could pick up the bodies," Sergeant Watkins said. "We can hardly send them down on the train with the tourists." He put a hand on Evan's shoulder. "Maybe you should go to the inn where they reported the missing climber and find out who he was, and bring the manager down to HQ to make a positive ID on him."

"He's not going to like that very much," Evan said, grinning.

"Difficult chap, is he?" Sergeant Watkins asked with the ghost of a grin.

"Let's put it this way. He acts as if he bloody owns the mountains," Evan said.

"And I tell you what, constable," the detective said. "If we get them down and find out that they are both missing heirs to the same fortune, then we'll take the matter further, okay?"

"Fair enough, sarge," Evan said.

There had to be a connection, he thought. Somehow he was determined to find it.

Chapter 4

After leaving Detective Sergeant Watkins as he put in his call to headquarters, Evan made his way back down the mountain to Llanfair, taking the Pig Track, the steeper but quicker of the two main paths. Even for someone as fit as Evan it was a good hour's scramble down the mountain past the Bwlch y Moch, the pass of pigs. But that was just as fast as waiting for the next train down the other side on the cog railway to Llanberis. Besides, he was glad to be alone for a while. It gave him time to think. Seeing that body last night still had him feeling shaken up. And the realization this morning that the whole thing was maybe not an accident had disturbed him even more.

He glanced back at the spot where he knew one of the bodies lay, and picked out the only ledge from which the man could have fallen. What would anyone have been doing out there in the first place? Or on the first ledge, for that matter? Neither of them led to anywhere that couldn't be reached by an easier track. Neither afforded spectacular views for a special camera shot or led to great climbs. They were ordinary but steep, out-of-the-way bits of the mountain and the fact that two people had fallen to their death from them convinced Evan that something strange was going on.

It was still early in the day for hikers, but even so, Evan was surprised not to see a living soul on this side of the mountain. He paused and glanced over his shoulder uneasily. He had been alone on the mountain all his life and usually he enjoyed the solitude and the feeling of being, literally, on top of the world. Today he was very conscious of his isolation. There was a tension in the air, almost as if the mountain itself was alert and watchful. Evan found himself thinking of Druids. He'd read once that they used to sacrifice people in high places. Didn't they throw their victims to their deaths? He shivered. A madman running around on the mountain, that's what Sergeant Watkins had said, wasn't it? Maybe he was right.

He fought the desire to break into a run as he dropped down the last slope and crossed Llyn Llydaw by the causeway. The sight of familiar landmarks and the village of Llanfair lying below reassured him. He slowed his step and looked back at the mountain, trying to notice any clue that he could give to Sergeant Watkins.

The causeway had been built long ago when there had been copper mines on the mountain's flanks and they needed a safe, speedy route for the donkeys carrying the ore down to the road. What an improbable undertaking Evan thought, glancing back at the mountain. How could they ever have made it profitable, carrying out the ore one sack at a time?

The Everest Inn rose up to meet him, its gingerbread balconies shining in the harsh sunlight. The rain was only an hour or so away now, Evan decided. He could detect the salt tang on the breeze. He hoped they got those bodies out before it set in. When it started raining in Wales, there was no knowing when it would stop again and once the cloud came down, there was no way they could get a helicopter anywhere near either body.

"Nasty business, constable," Major Anderson said, sucking through his teeth again in a way that Evan was beginning to find annoying. "Damn tragic." For a moment Evan nodded with sympathy until he went on, "Can you imagine what this will do for the inn? We've been trying to promote ourselves as a family vacation site. Nobody is going to want to bring their children to a place where people fall off mountains."

Evan nodded and kept quiet. No sense in voicing his suspicions to the major.

"And to think that the whole thing could have been avoided too," Major Anderson went on, glancing up from his desk at Evan.

"How do you figure that, major?"

"If a search party had gone up when I first requested help . . ."

"Then we could have stopped him from falling, is that what you're saying?" Evan demanded.

"It's possible." The major's red face turned a shade redder. "He could have been stuck somewhere, clinging to a rock face, yelling for help, getting weaker and weaker until his hands wouldn't hold him any more."

"Not in this case, major," Evan said. "If he'd been stuck on the rock face and yelled, someone would have looked up and seen him. If he'd let go, he would have slithered and bounced his way down and landed on his back or side. This man was lying on his front. He had fallen outward."

"Very strange," the major said.

"That's what we think," Evan said. "And of course, now we have to notify the next of kin. He filled in a registration slip when he arrived, I presume, and maybe we could take a look at his room."

"Oh yes, he'll be on our computer," Major Anderson said. "We're very modern here, you know. All automated."

He led Evan out of his office into the main lobby. Evan found it rather gloomy, with its wooden walls and dark carpets and oversized river-rock fireplace, but it was obvious that a lot of money had gone into it.

"Here we are. Alison will find his record for you," the major said. "The missing climber—what was his name again?"

"You mean the man who didn't come back to room 42?" the young girl asked. Her fingers flew over the keyboard and a record appeared. "Mr. Thomas Hatcher," the girl read out. "Eighty-seven Milton Road, Kilburn, London."

"A Londoner, eh?" Evan said, because he felt that he needed to say something. "Do you have any record of his phone calls after he arrived?"

"I can't see what his phone calls have to do with falling off a mountain," Major Anderson snapped.

"We're just trying to trace the friend he said he was going to meet," Evan said calmly.

"Ah." The major's face relaxed. "We only log calls out and he didn't make any, I'm afraid."

"Too bad," Evan said. "Maybe we could take a look at his room now. It's always good to know who we're contacting before we send someone blundering in to announce a death to the family."

"Er, quite," Major Anderson said. "Key to number 42, please, Alison."

Evan got the impression that Major Anderson had been

38

hired as a figurehead. He probably wasn't too good with the day-to-day details needed to run a hotel. Alison's quietly long-suffering look confirmed this. "Here you are, major," she said. "Room 42 is up the main staircase on the right."

"I know where it is," Major Anderson snapped. "Follow me, please."

He led Evan up an impressive wooden staircase to a carpeted upper hallway. Room 42 had a view of the pass with just a glimpse of the ocean beyond. A first glance conveyed that Thomas Hatcher was a neat man. Folded pajamas lay on the bed. An electric shaver and toothbrush were beside the wash basin, otherwise there was no sign that the room had been used.

"He didn't bring much stuff with him, did he?" Evan asked. He opened a top drawer and saw a neatly folded sweater, underclothes, and socks.

"He probably has his wallet with him with all the details you'd need," Major Anderson said. "You'll know more when you get him out."

"Probably," Evan agreed. He opened the closet. A jacket was hanging there and Evan went through the pockets. "Hullo," he said, drawing out a slim plastic wallet from the inside pocket. "Now that's very interesting." He flashed the laminated card at the major. "Metropolitan Police. The man was in the force."

Evan looked forward to seeing Sergeant Watkins' face when he told him that one of the victims was a London policeman. Now the detective would have to take the case more seriously, wouldn't he? All sorts of scenarios came to mind as he drove the silent major down to Bangor to identify the body. At first he thought that the major was reluctant to come with him because it was taking up his valuable time. Now it occurred to him that the major was definitely looking pale as they approached Bangor. Maybe he wasn't relishing the thought of having to look at a battered body. Maybe his branch of the army hadn't actually seen any real fighting!

Evan couldn't help grinning to himself as he turned the car into the yard outside police headquarters in Bangor.

"I've got the major in the waiting room," Evan said when he located Sergeant Watkins in his cubicle.

"So he came without a fight, did he?" Sergeant Watkins asked.

"Yes, but he's looking a trifle green," Evan said. "Did they manage to get the bodies out yet?"

"Yes, they're here. The police surgeon's already taken a look at them. He puts the time of death sometime late afternoon for both of them. The cause of death was extensive trauma, in case you're wondering if they were drugged or poisoned first."

"You still think there were two separate accidents, don't you?" Evan asked.

Sergeant Watkins nodded. "And I'm going to go on thinking it because we'd never have a way of proving otherwise."

"And if I told you that the man from the inn, Thomas Hatcher, was a copper from London? You don't see any significance in that?"

Sergeant Watkins shook his head. "And if I told you that the other bloke was a burglar alarm salesman from Liverpool? We've spoken to his wife and she's getting someone to drive her over to identify the body. Her husband had the only car with him. We've found it parked in the lot up at the cog railway station.

"What about the other dead man?" Evan asked. "Did she know whether her husband was going to meet him?"

"She didn't even know he was going to Wales," Watkins replied. "You can stick around and ask her yourself, if you are interested."

"Thanks, sarge," Evan said.

"You don't have to thank me," Sergeant Watkins said. "You'd be doing me a favor if you took her off my hands. I can't stand hysterical women. If I have her and her little kids crying all over me, it gets me started too." He paused reflectively. "Sometimes I wonder if I'm in the right job."

Evan nodded in understanding. His mind flashed back to a grave site, standing surrounded by all those blue uniforms, trying to look in control and professional when all he wanted to do was to yell and punch somebody.

"So she's coming here later today, is she?" Evan asked.

"Yes, she said she'd try and find someone to give her a ride, but it could take a while. And it's a good two-hour drive from Liverpool, isn't it?"

"I don't think I can stick around that long," Evan said. "I've got to drive the major straight back to Llanfair, haven't I?"

"I'll give you a call when she gets here if you like," Watkins said. "Strictly unofficial, of course."

"Of course." Evan was thinking that he might have underestimated the colorless Sergeant Watkins. "So what was his name then, this other man?" he asked.

"Stewart Potts," Sergeant Watkins said with only the ghost of a smile.

41

"Stew Potts? It's a wonder he didn't change it. I bet he got teased about it at school," Evan commented. "Don't tell me his wife's name's Honey?"

"Greta," Sergeant Watkins said. "Sounds foreign. And she didn't sound too upset over the phone. Of course it takes awhile to sink in sometimes, doesn't it?"

"Yes," Evan said. "It does."

"Well, I suppose we'd better go and take your major to identify the body," Sergeant Watkins said. "We might as well get this over with as quickly as possible."

Major Anderson's face was set grimly as he followed Watkins and Evan down to the morgue. Evan noticed that he swallowed hard as the attendant pulled out the drawer containing the body.

"Yes," Major Anderson said after he had stared long and hard at the body. "I think that's the man who was staying at the Inn. Of course, I can't be one hundred percent sure in the circumstances."

"Quite," Sergeant Watkins said, looking down at the battered and bruised face.

"But definitely same build, same hair color. Poor chap," he added. "Rotten way to end, what?"

"Did you know he was a policeman, Major Anderson?" Sergeant Watkins asked as the attendant shut the drawer again.

"We found out when the constable and I went through his things," Major Anderson said.

"So he hadn't mentioned it before?"

"No, why on earth should he?" Major Anderson said sharply. He glanced at his watch. "If we're through here, I really should be getting back. I've got important guests arriving at three and I should be there to welcome them."

He sat drumming his fingers on his knee and staring out of the window in stony silence as Evan drove him home.

"That's him all right," Greta Potts said as Evan showed her the photo taken on the mountain. It hadn't been easy for her to identify the corpse. His face had been pretty well smashed by the fall and she couldn't bring herself to take a good look. "I'd know those shoes anywhere," she added in disgust. "I was that mad at him when he came home with them. Almost a hundred pounds for shoes, I said to him when I found the box in the closet. Me and the children could have bought ourselves enough clothes for the summer with that money. But he said he had to have them—I didn't expect him to go barefoot, did I?" Her accent was an interesting mix of foreign overlaid with the flat vowel sounds of Liverpool. "That was Stew all over," she added. "He liked to treat himself well."

She looked at Evan with her lip curled in a sneer. She was light-haired in a Germanic sort of way with sharp angular features, and she wore far too much makeup. She was dressed in a shiny neon green blouse over a tight, short black skirt and she wore very high heels. As she spoke she got out a packet of cigarettes and nervously tapped one into her hand. "You don't mind, do you?" she stated, rather than asked. Evan didn't imagine she'd been very easy to live with.

"So he didn't say anything to you about going to the mountains?" Evan asked gently.

"He never told me where he was going. If he said he was going to climb a mountain, I'd have thought that was just another excuse."

"Excuse for what?"

The lip curled again. "My Stewart fancied himself as a ladies' man. You know how sailors have a girl in every port?

43

Salesmen are the same. He had a big territory. Sometimes he was gone all week. Who knows what he got up to? I should never have married him and come to this godforsaken country."

"Where did you two meet?" Evan asked.

"He was stationed in my home town in Germany when he was in the army," Greta said. "I met him at a dance. He was a wonderful dancer—good looking too." She rummaged in her purse and pulled out a snapshot of a tall, dark-haired man with his arm around her shoulder. "I should have listened to my mother and stayed home."

"Will you go back there now, do you think?" Evan asked.

She shrugged. "I don't know. I've got the kids to think of, haven't I? And we've got a nice little house in Liverpool. I don't know."

"Of course you don't," Evan said. "Take your time to let this all sink in before you make any decisions."

"What are you, a bloody therapist?" she snapped.

He glanced down at the photo again. "Mind if I keep this for a while?"

"What for?" she asked suspiciously.

Evan didn't want to voice his suspicions to her. "We're still trying to work out where he fell from and how," he said. "Someone might have passed him up on the mountain."

"What was he doing up on a bloody mountain, that's what I want to know," Greta demanded.

"So you say he wasn't usually the outdoor type?"

"Stew? Outdoors? Don't make me laugh," she said, not smiling. "The only time he went outdoors was to watch Liverpool play football on Saturday afternoons. He was a great Liverpool supporter. He lived for his football. I used to say to

him, if you loved these kids half as much as you love those bloody football players . . ."

"And you never heard him mention a friend called Thomas Hatcher? A friend from London?"

She frowned, then shook her head. "No, I never heard that name before. I didn't know he had any friends in London. Was that who he went to meet?"

"He didn't tell you he was going to meet a friend then?"

"I told you," she said impatiently, "he didn't tell me anything. I thought he'd probably left on the Sunday because he had to make a presentation early Monday morning. He did that sometimes. Anyway, he'd never have told me he was going to meet a friend—he knew I'd never have believed it was a bloke." She sighed. "Anyhow he's gone now and I shouldn't be speaking ill of the dead, should I? Poor old Stew. He was in Northern Ireland for a time in the army and he came through that all right, and now this. Doesn't seem fair, does it?"

For the first time Evan noticed the crack in her armor and thought that maybe the cold aggressiveness might be a defence mechanism to show that she wasn't about to mourn a womanizing husband. He put his hand on her shoulder. "Come on, love. I'll buy you a cup of tea," he said softly.

Chapter 5

Dark clouds were racing in from the ocean as Evan drove back to the village around four o'clock. Just as he was getting out of his car the bus pulled up and disgorged a load of school children from the comprehensive school down in Portmadog.

" 'Ello, Constable Evans, Sut ywt ti? 'Ow are you?" they called out in their clear lilting voices in the mixture of Welsh and English that they most often used.

Evan waved back as he headed for his door.

"Mr. Evans?"

Evan turned back to see Dilys Thomas, a gangly thirteen-year-old.

"What is it, Dilys?" Evan asked and watched her blush crimson.

"Did you hear that we're having a teen dance on Saturday?" she asked, playing with a long strand of hair to hide her embarrassment.

"I did hear something about it, yes," Evan said. "Going to

be one of those rave things, isn't it? All wild music and flashing lights?"

"Oh no, nothing like that," Dilys exclaimed in horror, not realizing he was pulling her leg. "It's in the chapel hall. I was wondering if you were going to be one of the chaperons?"

"I said I might," Evan said, "but I'm not so sure I can make it now. I've got a lot of things on my plate this week."

Dilys' face fell. "Oh, but you have to come," she said. "I was hoping you'd dance with me once."

"You've never seen me dance," Evan said, laughing. "Anyhow, you'll have the boys lining up to dance with you. I won't get a look in."

"No, they won't," Dilys said, her face still very red. "They make fun of me because I'm taller than they are. They call me Telephone-pole Thomas."

"I wouldn't worry if I were you," Evan said. "That will all sort itself out soon enough. But I'll try my best to come to the dance and I promise I'll dance with you if I'm there, okay?"

"Thanks, Mr. Evans," Dilys said. She gave him a dazzling smile. "Bye now. I have to get home or my ma will kill me."

Evan watched her run off, marvelling at her innocence. Why couldn't childhood be like that for all kids, he thought, her biggest worry that she had grown before the boys of her age. How come some lives were trouble-free and others were cut short by tragedy? It didn't seem fair and it didn't make sense. Evan liked things to make sense.

"Are you not speaking to me today then?" A soft, smooth voice made him jump. Then it was his turn to blush. "Oh, Bronwen, I'm sorry, I didn't notice you. I was thinking."

"That's all right. I forgive you," she said, and gave him a smile that warmed him right down to his boots. "So they let

48

you go hiking on work days now, do they? I saw you coming down the track through the classroom window."

"I'll have you know I've been up that bloody mountain twice within the last twenty-four hours," Evan said, a little put out. "Once last night and then again first thing this morning. And it wasn't too pleasant, either."

"I know—the climbing accident," she said. "I was only teasing because I imagine it can't have been too nice for you, getting out a body."

"It wasn't just one body," Evan said. "It was two."

"Two? Were they roped together?"

"No, it wasn't even the same accident."

"That's very strange." Bronwen shielded her eyes to gaze upward at the peak. "You and I were both up there yesterday and I'd have said it was perfect weather for climbing or walking. No excuse for falling, was there?"

"Like you say, it was very strange," Evan said. "Sergeant Watkins thinks it was just a horrible coincidence."

"And you don't?"

"I'm still thinking about it," Evan said. "One man's wife came today to identify him. I expect the other man's next of kin will show up soon enough. Maybe we'll know more then."

"You look tired," Bronwen said. "Long day, huh?"

"And I've only had a packet of crisps and a cup of tea since seven," Evan said. "I could eat a horse right now."

"I got the impression that was what Mrs. Williams had in mind for your tea," Bronwen said, smiling. "I met her in the shop and she was very upset that you'd missed your lunch. She seems to think you're about to waste away any moment."

Evan gave an embarrassed smile. "I feel like a prize turkey being fattened up for Christmas sometimes," he said. "I keep

49

telling her I don't need lunch but she cooks it anyway, and it's there, dry and nasty on a plate in the oven, waiting for me whenever I show up."

"That's one of the problems with landladies," Bronwen said.

"She means well and she's good-hearted enough," Evan said. "It's just this food thing, and her granddaughter."

"Her granddaughter?"

"Sharon," Evan said. "She seems to think we'd be a good match."

"Everyone in this place is determined to get you married off," Bronwen said, giving a nervous laugh.

"Don't worry, I intend to take my own good time about that," Evan answered.

"So I've noticed," Bronwen said under her breath. Then out loud she said, "Well, I best be getting along now and leave you to finish up your work and get home for your tea. I'll be seeing you then, Evan Evans."

"Right-o, Bronwen. Take care now," Evan said.

He let himself into the little room in the end cottage that served as the police station. It was next to Roberts-the-Pump, the gas station and repair shop which also served as the local fire station, RAC facility, and snack shop. A light was flashing on his answering machine. He punched the button. "This is Mrs. Powell-Jones," an impatient, stridently upper-class voice said. "Constable Evans, I've been trying to contact you all day on a matter of great urgency. Please come up to the house as soon as you return."

Evan sighed. He doubted if it was a real emergency. Mrs. Powell-Jones, wife of the reverend who preached his sermons in both languages, was one of those autocratic, well-born women who think that the term public servant is to be taken literally. She never hesitated to call Evan if her cat was missing at two in the morning or if she saw something she thought looked suspicious—and Mrs. Powell-Jones found a lot of things suspicious, like a young couple parked with the engine idling at midnight. But he knew he had to go. Mrs. Powell-Jones had friends in high places, like the major. He didn't want to risk facing an angry commissioner of police in the morning.

The Powell-Jones' house was the last house in the village, set back in spacious grounds, conveniently close to chapel Beulah. It had been inherited from Mrs. Powell-Jones' family, who had formerly owned the slate quarry. With its Victorian gables and turret in one corner, it contrasted strongly with the simple cottages below it. Personally Evan preferred the cottages.

Mrs. Powell-Jones herself opened the front door. She looked agitated; her normally neat waves of hair were in disarray as if she had been running her hands through them.

"Thank God you've come at last, constable," she said. "I was terrified you wouldn't get here in time." Her voice had a hint of Welsh lilt to it, but was overlaid with expensive English schooling.

"In time for what, Mrs. Powell-Jones?" Evan asked. "Got a problem, have you?"

"A problem?" she shrieked. "A crime has been committed here, constable."

"If there was a crime then you should have called down to headquarters," Evan said. "Didn't you hear the instructions on my answering machine? When I'm not in the office they page me or pick up my emergency calls. They'd have had someone up here in a jiffy."

"It's not the sort of crime I care to entrust to strangers," Mrs. Powell-Jones said, glancing around in case someone was listening. "Come out to the garden now, quickly, before it starts raining and the evidence is washed away."

Mystified, Evan followed her out to her back garden. The predicted rain was already beginning, a fine mist which clung like diamonds to Mrs. Powell-Jones' gray-streaked hair. It was a large garden surrounding the house, protected from the fierce winds by a high hedge. First came a lawn, surrounded by neatly kept rose beds, then another hedge, and beyond that a vegetable garden, where the property stretched up to meet the grounds of the Everest Inn. The inn itself loomed like a giant surreal shadow in the mist, making Evan shiver.

"Look you!" Mrs. Powell-Jones said dramatically pointing at the ground. Evan looked but wasn't sure what he was supposed to be looking at. It was all newly dug earth with some sorry-looking bits of green stalk sticking out of it at crazy angles.

"What exactly happened?" he asked at last.

"That's what I want you to find out," Mrs. Powell-Jones said. "Of course I have my suspicions. She's eaten up with jealousy that I beat her every year at the show."

"The show?" Evan was becoming more confused by the second.

"The flower and vegetable show down in Beddgelert," Mrs. Powell-Jones said. "I've won first place with my tomatoes for the past three years. So this year somebody decided to take matters into their own hands and sabotage my tomatoes before they could get going."

"Tomatoes?" Evan wasn't much of a gardener.

Mrs. Powell-Jones pointed at the little bits of plant lying on the soil. "Those were my prize tomato seedlings until yesterday," she said. "Someone has deliberately trampled them in a vicious act of vandalism."

"And you think you know who did it?" Evan asked.

"Of course. Mrs. Parry Davies. Who else would it be? I just happen to do most things better than her and she can't stand it," she said triumphantly.

Evan was examining the soil. It contained the print marks of large boots with a marked tread.

"Mrs. Parry Davies wears a size twelve in boots, does she?" he asked.

"Of course not. Don't be ridiculous," Mrs. Powell-Jones said.

"Then I'd say she wasn't the leading suspect," Evan said. "Look at the size of these boot marks."

"Oh." For a second she was speechless, then a smile lit her face again. "A clever ploy, so that I wouldn't suspect her. After all, she does play all the character parts in the local dramatic society, and her husband does have very big feet. Go and confront her with the evidence, constable. Mark my words, she'll break down and confess."

"I can hardly go and . . ." Evan began. "After all, we don't know that . . . I mean it would hardly be fair to . . ."

"Who else could it be, man?" Mrs. Powell-Jones exclaimed. Evan was beginning to understand why her husband gave such long sermons. It kept him out of the house an extra half hour. "Nobody else wishes my tomatoes to fail, except for her. I am most generous with my garden produce. Everyone in the village is amply supplied with the bounty of my garden. And it was just the tomatoes, mark you. The vandal didn't hit my brussel sprouts, did she?"

Evan thought privately that it might have been a blessing if the vandal hadn't overlooked the brussels sprouts. His landlady didn't believe in wasting anything and would cook them, night after night, if Mrs. Powell-Jones donated them. Evan had never liked brussels sprouts.

"I'll do what I can, Mrs. Powell-Jones," Evan said. "I'll try and clear the matter up for you."

"Make sure that you do, constable," Mrs. Powell-Jones said. "Make it your number-one priority. Vandalism can't be allowed to flourish, can it?"

Evan gave a little half bow and beat a hasty retreat. He glanced longingly at the swinging sign on the Red Dragon. After a long and trying day a good pint was just what he needed, but he still had paperwork to catch up on, and he wanted to do some more thinking about those two men who had plunged to their deaths.

Through a knothole in the shed door, a pair of eyes watched Mrs. Powell-Jones go back into her house. When the front door closed behind her, a sigh of relief escaped through clenched teeth and the pickax was slowly lowered. A grin slowly spread across the thin lips. People really were so stupid!

Chapter 6

"Go on in, constable," the friendly young police-woman at the front desk said to Evan when he arrived at headquarters the next morning. "Sergeant Watkins has got Thomas Hatcher's mother here to see the body. He's expecting you."

Evan had driven down right away in response to a phone call. The more he thought about the two accidents, the more he was convinced he was not wrong in his first suspicion. Scotland Yard hadn't been helpful. It turned out that Thomas Hatcher was only an ordinary copper on the beat and not, as Evan had hoped, an undercover cop pursuing some secret assignment on the mountain. He hoped Thomas Hatcher's mother might reveal something, because Sergeant Watkins was clearly anxious to close this case and release the bodies for burial.

She looked up as he came into the room, a small, skinny woman with a sharp cockney face and even sharper eyes. She was clearly wearing her Sunday best—a wool coat that had once been black, now faded to brownish gray, and a small black hat. She clutched a large black purse and her umbrella defiantly to her.

"You were the one who found my Tommy, was yer?" she asked.

Evan nodded. "I'm very sorry, Mrs. Hatcher. It must be a nasty shock for you."

Mrs. Hatcher nodded and Evan noticed that her fingers clenched and unclenched around the handle of her purse, even though her face remained impassive and her eyes dry. "He was a good boy," she said. "A good son, too."

"Did he live with you?" Evan asked.

She shook her head. "No, he had his own place, but he came over to visit regular, once a month. Always tried to come to Sunday dinner and never forgot my birthday. He was a good boy."

"Did he do a lot of walking and climbing? Was that his hobby?" Evan asked.

The small, sharp eyes opened wider. "Not that I ever heard of. He had his motorbike, of course. That was his main hobby—always working on it, he was. He loved that bike. But I've never heard he had any interest in mountain climbing. Of course, he liked excitement. He might have gone if one of his friends suggested it."

"Did he have a lot of friends?"

"Oh yes. Everyone liked Tommy," she said.

"Ever hear him talk of a friend called Stewart? Stew Potts? Funny old name, isn't it?"

The face registered no change of expression. "I can't say I ever heard that name. Of course, he was always close—never told me much, even when he was a little kid. I used to say

56

"How was school?" and he'd say "All right." That's all I ever got out of him."

"So he didn't tell you why he was going to North Wales for the weekend?"

"He never even told me he was going," she said. "You could have knocked me down with a feather when the policeman came to the door. I didn't believe it was my Tommy, not until I saw the body . . ." Her voice trailed away into silence. "It seems such a waste, don't it?" she said in a cracked voice. "He was doing so well. He was so happy now. He'd got a nice girlfriend and he loved being a policeman. We were all so glad he'd finally found something he wanted to do with his life. We all knew he'd made a mistake going into the army, but you can't tell a seventeen-year-old anything, can you? They always know better."

She got to her feet. "I best be getting along then. I've got a train to catch. They'll tell me when I can make the funeral arrangements, will they?"

"Yes, they'll be in touch," Evan said. "And Mrs. Hatcher, if you take a look in his flat and you find anything that would give us a hint what he was doing here, let me know, will you?" He scribbled his phone number and address on a sheet of paper.

"You think there's something wrong, don't you?" she asked, the sharp eyes darting around the room.

"We're . . . not sure," he said. "Let's just say we'd like to look into it further."

"I'll give yer any help I can, constable," she said. "I don't like to think that my Tommy died for nothing."

Evan escorted her to the door and watched her thank everyone politely as she walked out with great dignity.

"Any closer to solving the great mystery?" Sergeant Watkins came up behind him. "They didn't know each other, did they? No connection?"

"As a matter of fact there was a connection, sarge," Evan said. "They were both in the army."

"So were a lot of working-class lads, I should imagine," Sergeant Watkins said. "The army is one of the few jobs in high unemployment areas like Liverpool, isn't it? And I wouldn't be surprised if they were both in the Boy Scouts too, and that they both went to comprehensive schools and they both liked football!"

"But it wouldn't hurt to check their army records, would it?" Evan asked. "See if their paths ever crossed?"

"And what then?" Sergeant Watkins demanded. "Even if they knew each other, we're still only guessing that some kind of foul play was involved, aren't we? And even if someone pushed them both off the mountain, how are you going to prove it?"

"You could start by asking some questions," Evan said. "A lot of people must have been up there yesterday."

Sergeant Watkins ran his hand through his hair. "Look Evans, this isn't bloody Scotland Yard, you know. If I ask my chief to start a full investigation, we take men off that little girl's murder. Do you want me to do that?"

"I see it was in this morning's paper," Evan said, pointing to the latest edition of the *Daily Post* that lay on the sergeant's desk. TRADEDY STRIKES TWICE ON MOUNTAIN PEAK was the banner headline. "In a corner of the world already reeling from the brutal murder of a young girl earlier this week, tragedy has struck again, claiming the lives of two men on Mt. Snowdon (Yr Wyddfa). Killed in separate climbing accidents were . . ." Evan looked up. "Maybe that will jog someone's memory and make them come forward. And would you have any objection to my getting their records from the army—just to satisfy myself?"

"I can see that life as a village policeman must be deadly dull," Sergeant Watkins said. "What you do in your own time is up to you, constable, but I'm not giving you any official clearance to look into crimes that may or may not have happened. For one thing, I think it's a total waste of time. For another, I don't have the authority. I'm only a humble sergeant, you know. And it's not like we're bloody Scotland Yard up here. My chief has got the national press breathing down his neck to solve this little girl's murder. It would be more than my job's worth to waste another minute on these climbing accidents—which is what I'm calling them until someone can prove otherwise."

"Okay, sarge, keep your hair on," Evan said good-naturedly, then realized this was probably an unwise turn of phrase, seeing that the sergeant was already getting thin on top and could very well be sensitive about it. "I've heard D.C.I. Caldwell's a bugger to work for."

Watkins nodded. "So's Detective Inspector Hughes, who's my immediate boss. Believes in solving crimes like Sherlock Holmes from clues like burnt matches and bits of paper. Everyone's a bit edgy about catching this Lou Walters."

"I understand, sarge," Evan said. "But I can't see what harm it could do if I pursued my own private investigations, as they say. If it turns out to be a big spy plot, you can buy me a beer," he added, giving the detective sergeant a challenging grin.

"I don't mind doing that," Sergeant Watkins said. "And if you turn up nothing, then you can buy me one."

The two men shook hands and Evan hurried out to his car.

He hadn't exactly got a go-ahead, but he hadn't outright been told to mind his own business either. He'd have to see how and where one faxed the army. He imagined getting records wouldn't be that straightforward and he wanted to get started right away.

It was two o'clock when he let himself into his landlady's house in the village.

"Is that you, Mr. Evans?" a voice echoed down the narrow, dark passageway. Mrs. Williams came scurrying out of the kitchen, wiping her hands on the apron she wore every day except Sundays. She always asked the question, even though Evan was the only person with a key to let himself into her house.

He had been given Mrs. Williams' name when he first arrived, as a lady who took in summer visitors and would welcome some extra cash in the off-season. Mrs. Williams had made him comfortable and had shown no sign of wanting to turn him out, even when the summer visitors arrived, so he had stayed on. He knew he should find his own place but he was reluctant to come home to canned spaghetti and a cold room after having a landlady who was happy to do his washing and mending and feed him three square meals a day, not counting elevenses and tea if he came home at those times.

"Deed to goodness, where have you been again?" she demanded as if he was a naughty five-year-old. "It's past your dinnertime and a good shepherd's pie spoiled in the oven."

"I told you that you don't need to make lunch for me, Mrs. Williams," Evan said apologetically. "I am a policeman. I don't keep regular hours. Besides, I'm trying to eat light at lunchtime."

"Eat light?" Mrs. Williams sniffed. "You need to keep your strength up. Besides, girls like a man with a bit of meat on him. Our Sharon, for example. She thinks you're lovely. 'He's nice and chubby, isn't he?' That's what she said last time she was here."

Evan winced at being called nice and chubby and resolved to jog up the Snowdon track once a day until he had run off all of Mrs. Williams' added pounds.

"Don't stand there. Come on in," she said. "The pie's still hot in the oven and I've got turnips and parsnips to go with it."

Evan sighed and allowed himself to be led into the big, warm kitchen. The kitchen table was covered by a blue-and-white checkered cloth, which was scarcely visible under the various dishes that covered it. In the middle was a teapot hiding under a crocheted cozy in lurid red-and-orange stripes. Mrs. Williams kept hot tea going all day in case anyone dropped in for a chat. This was usual procedure for women of her age but happened less and less often these days. The younger women went to work or took classes instead of sitting around gossiping.

Next to the teapot was a bread board with a crusty new loaf on it. Next to that a cake stand with scones and slices of bara brith, the Welsh speckled bread, dotted with currants. On the other side was another cake stand with eccles cakes and iced fairy buns.

"Are you expecting company?" Evan asked suspiciously.

"Only you," Mrs. Williams said. "You missed your dinner and your tea yesterday." She still insisted on calling lunch dinner. "I wanted to make sure you had both today so I got the tea ready early. You can have your pie first and then your tea—oh and I've got an apple crumble in the oven with some fresh cream from Evans-the-Milk."

The promise of apple crumble and fresh cream was too much for Evan. He gave in to temptation and sat at the place prepared for him while Mrs. Williams fluttered around loading

61

his plate with rich, moist shepherd's pie, its potato crust nicely crisp on top. She accompanied this with generous helpings of mashed turnips and parsnips each topped with a large knob of butter.

"Did they find out any more about that treadful murder of the little girl?" she asked. *"Treadful"* was one of her favorite words. "And what about those two poor men who fell down the mountain? Treadful, that was too, wasn't it?"

"Nothing much yet, Mrs. Williams," Evan said, looking at the steaming mound of food in front of him and realizing that he somehow had to get through all this before Mrs. Williams would bring on the apple pie and cream.

"Treadful," she said again. "All these people dying and being murdered. What's happening to the world, that's what I'd like to know."

Evan couldn't answer this. He had only taken a couple of mouthfuls when the phone rang.

"Now who could that be?" Mrs. Williams asked in annoyance. She always said this, as if she expected the other occupant of the room to somehow know who was calling.

"Three two one seven," she said, in a haughty voice she reserved for phone answering and English tourists. "Oh, it's you, Mrs. Powell-Jones." Evan's heart sank. "He's just eating his dinner right now. An emergency, is it? Very well, I'll tell him."

She put down the phone. "You're wanted up at Mrs. Powell-Jones' right away. She said to tell you she's got more evidence that she's just found."

Evan got up, half glad to have an excuse not to eat the enormous helping of shepherd's pie. Maybe by the time he got back, the pie would be cold and he could confine himself to the bread and cakes instead. Mrs. Williams was known for her baking. Her eccles cakes won prizes every year.

"You hurry yourself back now," she called after Evan. "Don't let that woman go bossing you around. She gives herself too many airs and graces. Lady of the manor—that's what she thinks she is, just because her old dad used to own the quarry and she went to school in foreign parts."

Mrs. Powell-Jones was waiting for Evan by the front gate. She had a scarf around her head to protect her waves from the fine misty rain that was still falling, but she still managed to look the part of lady of the manor, in spite of the well-worn gardening clothes and muddy boots.

"A crucial piece of evidence has come up," she said. "I only spotted it a little while ago when I was about to weed the flower beds. Come this way, please."

Evan followed obediently, wondering if Mrs. Powell-Jones had found a telltale hairpin on the trampled tomatoes. He was surprised when she didn't head for the vegetable garden, but instead when around to the back of the house.

"There," she said, pointing to the bed by the bay window. "What do you make of that?"

This time the evidence was clear enough. A large studded footprint was in the middle of the flower bed.

"You don't have a gardener who wears boots like that?" Evan asked.

"Of course not," she snapped. "We only have old Mr. Wilkins once a week and he wears Wellingtons. There was an intruder in this garden, Mr. Evans—the same person who trampled my tomatoes is now spying into my house, and we both know who it is, don't we?"

"You've got me there, Mrs. Powell-Jones," Evan said.

"Mrs. Parry Davies, of course. Wearing her husband's boots to throw me off the scent."

"Why would she be spying in your windows?"

"It's obvious, isn't it? I won the embroidery section in the show last year and she came second. She wants to see what needlepoint I'm doing this year. She knows I work on it in the evenings in this very room." She glared at him fiercely. "Have you confronted her yet? Has she owned up to the tomatoes?"

"I—haven't had a chance yet, Mrs. Powell-Jones. I've been down at HQ on a big case all day."

"Then look lively and get to it, man," Mrs. Powell-Jones commanded. "Who knows what she'll try next. The woman is desperate, I tell you."

With Mrs. Powell-Jones watching his every move, Evan had no alternative. He knocked tentatively on the Parry Davies' front door. Mrs. Parry Davies looked the part of a minister's wife, but without the upper-class air of Mrs. Powell-Jones. Her tweed skirt and brownish twinset were well worn. Her face was devoid of makeup and topped with a sensibly short hairstyle. She also appeared to have a sense of humor and, to Evan's relief, found the whole thing mildly amusing.

"That woman—I think she's gone bananas," she said when Evan, cringing with embarrassment, managed to explain why he was there. "As if I'd want to trample her tomato plants. If winning the local show is the biggest thrill of her year, then good luck to her. And as far as spying on her embroidery . . . I think she should examine her own conscience in that matter. Last year she came over here a couple of months before the show. I had already started on a tapestry of an old English mill. Do you know what she did?"

"No," Evan said politely.

"She went out and got herself a tapestry with three windmills on it. Three, mark you. It only won because it was bigger than mine. That's one-upmanship for you!"

·   ·   ·

Evan left the Davies residence feeling as if he had gone two rounds in a boxing ring. He wished that the pub was open. He was just passing the front of the pub when he met Charlie Hopkins coming out of it.

"I thought it was two hours to opening time, Charlie," he called.

Charlie grinned, revealing gaps in his teeth. "I was just making a delivery, Constable Evans. I went down to the cash-and-carry in Caernarfon today and I picked up paper napkins and towels for old Harry at the pub. Doin' him a good turn, I was."

"And you came right out again without wetting your whistle, right?" Evan asked, spotting a telltale wisp of froth on Charlie's upper lip.

Charlie put his finger to his nose. "Them that asks no questions, don't get told no lies, that's what my old mother used to say," he said. "What were you doing up there." He nodded in the direction of the chapels. "Popping in for a quick prayer?"

"Mrs. Powell-Jones had a Peeping Tom," Evan said.

Charlie chuckled. "I can't think why anybody would want to spy on her," he said. "If I was going to peep anywhere, I can think of better windows—young Betsy, for example. I wouldn't mind watching her undress."

"It wasn't undressing the peeper was spying on," Evan said. "It was embroidery."

Charlie's lean frame shook with amusement. Evan laughed too, but then he grew serious again. "All the same, Charlie," he said. "There's no denying there's a bloody great footprint in her flower bed and a Peeping Tom is a Peeping Tom. Who'd want to do a thing like that?"

"Sounds to me like the sort of thing Daft Dai used to do," Charlie said.

"Daft Dai?" Evan was instantly alert.

"That was way before your time. He was well known around here. Used to go around peeping in windows and annoying people. I used to think he was harmless but they put him away in the end. He took to scaring tourists. He used to say the mountains belonged to him and nobody was allowed up there without his permission."

"Is that a fact?" Evan asked.

Charlie nodded. "In the end he waved a knife at someone and that was that. They put him away."

"And where is he now?"

"Still in the looney bin, I'd imagine," Charlie said. "If they'd let him out, we'd have seen him. You couldn't miss Daft Dai."

"See you at the pub later then, Charlie," Evan said. He hurried into his office and made a phone call.

"Sarge?" he said, trying to hide the excitement in his voice. "You know you said this might be the work of a madman? I think we've got a suspect. I want you to check on a bloke called Daft Dai. Apparently he was well known in these parts so I don't think you'd have too much trouble tracing him. He was put in a mental home for claiming the mountains belonged to him and threatening tourists."

"Was he now?" Sergeant Watkins actually sounded interested. "That would be the sort of person we're looking for— if we're looking for anyone, which it seems you are. I'll have him checked on then."

Evan put down the phone with satisfaction. Maybe they'd have the case closed quickly after all.

Chapter 7

When Evan entered the Red Dragon later that evening, he found the place in great excitement.

"I tell you, Mr. Harris, he pulled up at my petrol pump and before I could ask him whether he wanted premium or unleaded, he stuck a bloody great microphone in my face," Roberts-the-Pump was saying. "He asked me what I thought about the tragedy. I didn't have a clue what he was talking about."

"I hope you gave him an intelligent answer, man," Evans-the-Meat said. "You don't want Wales to look stupid on national television, do you?"

"What's this about national television?" Evan asked, breaking into the tight knot of men around the bar.

"The TV news was here earlier today," Evans-the-Meat said. "Asking about those two men who died on the mountain. They didn't ask me, unfortunately . . ."

"Or you would have told them it served the bloody English right for coming here where they're not wanted," Evans-the-Milk inserted getting a general laugh.

"You want to be careful about saying things like that," Charlie Hopkins warned. "People will start thinking you might have pushed them."

"He would have, if he was still fit enough to climb up the mountain," Evans-the-Milk said, grinning at Evans-the-Meat's large stomach and red face.

"So what else did the newsman want to know?" Evan asked, stepping in quickly to avert yet another fight.

"He was trying to get us to say that it was too dangerous up there and that maybe parts of the mountain should be off limits to all but certified climbers," Roberts-the-Pump said.

"I'd go along with that," Charlie Hopkins said. "It would save us a few trips up the mountain to fetch down idiots who have got themselves into trouble."

"They should start with Crib Goch," Evans-the-Meat said. "I can't even count of the number of people who have lost their nerve crossing Crib Goch."

"That's because he's run out of fingers and toes," said Evans-the-Milk, but this time everyone remained serious.

Charlie Hopkins was nodding. "I've seen grown men whimpering like babies up there. We've had to carry a couple of them back, haven't we boys?"

"I don't understand what's wrong with it," Cut-Price-Harry said. He was Charlie's young nephew who worked down at the cash-and-carry and thus had been given the nickname to differentiate him from Harry-the-Pub. "It's wider than the path to the pub and I've never seen anybody fall off that yet, even when they've had a drop too much."

Evan said nothing, but he could understand why people

froze on Crib Goch. The path went along the top of the ridge leading to the summit of Snowdon, and although it was wide and smooth enough, the ground fell away, a thousand feet sheer on either side. To some people it felt like walking a tightrope.

"Turn on the telly, Betsy," Evans-the-Meat called. "We don't want to miss seeing ourselves on the news, do we?"

"I think it's all very exciting." Betsy reached up to turn on the set above the bar. "I just wish they'd have interviewed me."

"And what would you know about mountain rescues then?" Cut-Price-Harry demanded.

"Nothing, but I might have been discovered by a film producer, mightn't I?" Betsy smoothed down her silky blouse. "I might have been the next Madonna."

Cut-Price-Harry spluttered. "You? Madonna?"

"And why not? I've got the looks!" Betsy said haughtily.

"Yeah, but could you stand up there and sing 'Like a Virgin' without blushing?" Cut-Price-Harry gave his uncle a wink.

"You're just sore because I wouldn't go to that dance with you, Harry Morgan," Betsy snapped.

"Coming up on the nine o'clock news," said a disembodied voice from the TV set. "Tragedy strikes twice in the Welsh mountains."

"There you are, that's us," Evans-the-Meat said, nudging his neighbors.

"This is exciting," Charlie Hopkins said. "It reminds me of that last time we had the newspeople here."

"What was that then, Charlie?" Evan asked, suddenly alert.

"It was before you came," Charlie said, looking at the other men for confirmation. "About six, seven years ago, wouldn't you say?"

The other men nodded.

"And what happened?" Evan asked. "Another climbing accident?"

"No, that wasn't it," Evans-the-Milk said. "They were having some kind of army training exercises on the mountain and some poor man froze to death. He got left behind somehow—twisted his ankle I think—and the weather turned nasty and they found him frozen next day. There was an awful fuss about it—they had an inquiry at the war office, so we heard."

"You might have read about it in the papers," Charlie said to Evan. "The place was swarming with reporters. About this time of year too, wasn't it?"

"That's right, because I remember everyone said it was a freak snowstorm, this late in the year," Roberts-the-Pump said.

"Local boy too, wasn't he?" another voice added.

"That's right. He came from Portmadog, if I remember right," Charlie Hopkins said.

"Then he should have known better," Evans-the-Meat said.

"Meaning what?" Evans-the-Milk demanded. "That he should have known his way around the mountain better?"

"No," said Evans-the-Meat. "That he shouldn't have joined the bloody English army in the first place."

The next day the phone rang as Evan was attempting to catch up with his paperwork.

"This is Tommy Hatcher's mum," the sharp cockney voice echoed down the line. "You asked me to call you if I saw anything in his room. I was turning the place out yesterday and I come across a postcard on his chest of drawers. It was a picture of Mount Snowdon."

"It was?" Evan felt his pulse quicken. "What did it say?"

"I'll read it to you," Mrs. Hatcher said. "The writing's not too good but I think it says 'We never got a chance to hold a memorial for Danny, did we? Meet you up there, May 5th, two o'clock.' "

"What was the name?" Evan asked.

"It wasn't signed," Mrs. Hatcher said, "And it had a London postmark."

"A memorial for Danny," Evan said speculatively. "Any idea who that was?"

"None at all," she answered. "Like I said, Tommy never told me much about what was going on in his life. When he was in the army he only wrote when he wanted me to send him a food parcel. He didn't think much of army food."

"Could you put the postcard in an envelope and mail it to me?" Evan couldn't think exactly what he might want it for, but it was one small step toward solving this thing. "And please call me again if you come up with anything else, any little thing."

"You think this memorial had something to do with why my Tommy died?" she asked sharply.

"I don't know, but I hope to find out, Mrs. Hatcher," Evan said.

His brain was racing as he put down the phone. A memorial for Danny? It couldn't just be coincidence, could it? He ran outside and saw Charlie Hopkins getting out of his delivery van.

"Charlie," he called. "What was the man's name?"

"What man?" Charlie looked confused.

"The soldier you told me about who froze to death on the mountain."

Charlie thought for a moment. "I can't quite . . . something biblical, I'm sure."

71

"Was it Danny something?"

Charlie's face lit up. "That sounds as if it could be right. Danny . . . Danny . . . something biblical. I'll give you a call if it comes back to me."

"Thanks, Charlie."

"What's this all about then, Evan bach?" Charlie demanded.

"I don't know yet."

"You think there's some connection with the two men on the mountain?"

Evan shrugged. "It's possible. One of them had received an invitation to a memorial for someone called Danny. I'm going to take a look and see what I can find down at HQ."

Without waiting for Charlie to say more, he ran to his car. There were old newspapers on microfilm down at headquarters. He knew the date and the approximate year. It shouldn't be too hard to find out more.

It took him a while to find the newspaper reference he was looking for. It hadn't been front page material, as Charlie Hopkins had suggested, and Evan had to go through May issues for two consecutive years on the microfilm before he found the article on the "Other News" page of the *Daily Post*. He could see why the story hadn't made the headlines. It had certainly been a big news day, elsewhere in the world. Saddam Hussein was sounding threats in Iraq, Margaret Thatcher was putting up a last stand battle for her political life as her opponents sought to topple her government, and there had been a big train robbery. Evan remembered that well enough. A gang of masked men had overpowered the engineer of the London to Dublin Irish Mail train and made off with a cool two million. Evan had been a new young policeman at the time when the alert to keep a close watch on the ports had been sent to their Swansea station. He had patrolled the dockland constantly on the lookout, hoping to be the one who caught the robbers trying to flee the country. But they'd been smarter than that. They'd taken off in a private plane and were now probably safely in Argentina or Brazil. In any case, the loot had never been recovered.

At last he spotted the small headline: MOUNTAIN EXERCISE ENDS IN TRAGEDY. Evan adjusted the focus on the screen so he could read more easily. "Tragedy occurred on the top of Mt. Snowdon last night when eighteen-year-old Private Danny Bartholemew froze to death during army survival training." It was just as Charlie had said. A group of soldiers from Caterick base in Yorkshire had been transported to Snowdonia for combined army–air force survival training exercises. Overnight there had been an unexpected storm which had caused blizzard conditions on the mountain peaks. Danny wasn't reported missing until the next day, when they found him frozen near the summit of Snowdon. The strange thing was that his pack, containing foul weather gear, survival blanket, emergency rations, whistle, and flashlight, was not with him. It wasn't found after an extensive search.

Evan pushed his chair back from the screen. He could understand that the poor boy had lost his pack. It could have come off if he'd lost his footing and fallen. Or he could have taken it off to get at his emergency supplies and the wind could have blown it over a cliff. Evan had known winds strong enough to do that. But then why was it never found? Had someone wanted to make sure that Danny Bartholomew died that night? And was it possible that his death was in some way linked to those of Tommy Hatcher and Stew Potts?

Chapter 8

The cramped living room looked as if it had been frozen in a time warp. The faded red flower print curtains were half drawn, shrouding the room in shadow. An open fireplace was still the only form of heating. A fire was laid in the grate but had not been lit recently and the room smelled damp and mildewy. The walls were papered in a different flower print and dotted with cheap reproductions of ships at sea. Every surface was cluttered with china dogs, horses, vases, photo frames. There was a fringed silky tablecloth on the table and crocheted antimacassars on the backs of the two uncomfortable-looking armchairs. To Evan it looked like a set from a BBC period piece. The room's only concession to modernity was the small TV set in the corner.

Curiosity had sent Evan in search of Danny's next of kin in Portmadog, the former slate port at the mouth of the Glaslyn River, but sitting opposite Danny's mother, he almost wished he had left well alone. The woman looked older than her years and belonged in the setting—herself a period piece from the fifties. She sat hunched in one of the arm chairs, her arms folded defiantly across her skinny chest, hair curlers peeping from under a scarf. She wore old satin slippers, through which a big toenail was peeping, and a sweater she had definitely knitted herself, and she smelled of stale booze and cigarette smoke. Evan could imagine her standing behind those heavy drapes, watching what went on outside.

"I don't know why you're raking this up again after all these years," she said, looking past Evan to the empty fireplace. "Haven't I suffered enough?"

"I'm very sorry, Mrs. Bartholemew," Evan said, "But you might have read about the two climbers who were killed over the weekend?"

"I don't read the papers and I don't watch the news," she said. "Only bad news always, isn't it?"

"Two men were killed on the mountain," Evan said.

"I don't know what that has to do with me," she said.

"It's just possible that they knew Danny," Evan said. "One of them got a postcard inviting him to a memorial for a person called Danny on May fifth. That was the day your Danny died, wasn't it?"

"I can't remember now," she said. "That would have been about right, I suppose. They didn't tell me until a couple of days later, but then the army never tells you anything, does it?"

"So I wondered if there was anything about your Danny and his time in the army," Evan went on. "Anything that might shed light on why these poor chaps died."

"I was against it from the start," she said, hugging her arms around herself now as if she was cold. " 'Why would you want to go fighting for the English?' I asked him. 'What have they ever done for us?' But he was so excited and proud. He was still only a boy, of course," she added and for a second her face lit up, so that Evan could see that she might once have been a handsome woman. "And I suppose it did mean a way of seeing the world to him. What else is there to do here, now that they've closed the quarries and the docks? Work as a bloody waiter in one of the posh hotels, if the Italians and Spaniards haven't taken all the jobs first. My Danny wanted to make something of his life . . . and look where it got him. Dead before his nineteenth birthday."

"Did he tell you much about his life in the army?" Evan asked gently. "Did you ever meet any of his mates?"

"Mates?" she asked, her voice sharp with bitterness again. "What kind of mates would leave a boy to freeze on a mountain? Mates look out for each other, don't they? My Danny didn't have any mates, and if he did, they let him down."

Evan started to get to his feet. He could see that Mrs. Bartholemew wasn't going to be much help and he was beginning to feel uneasy in that room, as if the walls were closing in on him. Maybe it was the hostile, defiant way that Mrs. Bartholemew glanced up at him from time to time, but he felt as tense as a wound watch spring.

"And you know what the English army wrote to me?" she demanded. "They said that I could be proud of him and that he was a good soldier, ready to serve his country. His country—the nerve of it. The bloody English always take and never give back."

"I'd best be getting on my way then," Evan said, heading for the door. "I won't take up any more of your time, Mrs. Bartholemew."

"So you're saying that those men might have been Danny's mates?" she asked, making him turn around. "Then I say serve them right. They got what was coming to them. They left my Danny in the lurch and they got what they deserved."

A movement in the passageway outside made Evan start. He thought he saw a shadow flit past. As he watched the door slowly opened and a cat walked in. Mrs. Bartholemew scooped it up. "There you are, puss. Where have you been, naughty girl? Out all night again, is it?"

"Do you live here alone, Mrs. Bartholomew?" Evan asked.

"Of course I live alone. I've got nobody now, have I? Those English took all my men away. My husband and my boys—all gone."

"Thanks for your help then, Mrs. Bartholomew," Evan said awkwardly. "I can see myself out. Give me a call if you can think of anything that might help us."

His gaze fell on one of the photos in a carved wood frame—two skinny little boys standing together on the beach beside an enormous sand castle. "Are these your boys?" Evan asked.

Danny's mother picked up the photo. "That was taken on holiday in Aberystwyth, the year before their daddy died. Worked to death, he was, by those English at the slate quarry. It was too much for his heart. Who'd have thought it would all end like this with me all alone here?" She held the photo close to her. "Damn those English. I'd never lift a finger to help them. Never," she said with venom in her voice. "They took both my sons from me. May they rot in hell."

"What happened to your other boy?" Evan ventured.

"The English took him too," she said bitterly. "Both my sons and my man too."

She sat hugging herself in such obvious grief he felt he'd be crass to prolong the interview. He wasn't going to get any more useful information out of her anyway.

"I'll be going then," he said quietly. He let himself out and stood for a moment on the street outside, breathing in the good salty air. He wished he had never bothered to visit Mrs. Bartholomew. He had learned nothing and had only opened old wounds for her. He realized that she hadn't even offered him a cup of tea.

When Evan arrived back at the police station in Llanfair, the light was flashing on his answering machine. Please not Mrs. Powell-Jones again, he prayed. But Sergeant Watkins' crisp voice came on the line instead. "I thought you might like to know that we've traced your Daft Dai. His name is David Morgan Davies, oringially from Caernarfon and he was released from the Royal Chester Mental Hospital in February," he said. "There's some possibility he's been seen in the area. We're trying to check on his current whereabouts. I'll let you know if we find out more. You might mention to your mountain rescue lads to keep an eye out for him, if any of you are up on the mountain. With any luck we'll have this business wrapped up in a couple of days."

Evan picked up the phone and put it down again. He wondered if he should call Sergeant Watkins and bring him up to date with the postcard and his other line of inquiry. Better to wait until he could present a really solid theory to the sergeant, he decided. He didn't want to be laughed at again for trying to play detective, and he hadn't any real facts to go on yet. He decided that maybe Sergeant Watkins was better occupied throwing all of his energy into catching the child murderer. Evan would quietly go on with his snooping until someone told him to stop.

He dialled directory enquiries and asked for the number of Caterick army base in Yorkshire. Ten frustrating minutes later he put down the phone. He had suspected that dealing with the army wasn't going to be easy, but this had been just like running into a brick wall. No, they couldn't look up personnel files without written authorization. No, he couldn't speak to the base commander. He'd have to get a clearance from the War Office first before they released anything, and he couldn't imagine the war office giving away anything to a mere village copper.

The interview with Mrs. Bartholomew and the subsequent frustrating phone call made him decide he needed to clear his head in the fresh air. There was no other business that couldn't wait. The village street was quiet. All seemed peaceful in Llanfair and nobody would miss the village copper if he took a quick hike up onto the mountain. He had the added excuse of being instructed to keep an eye out for Daft Dai, although he didn't think that even Daft Dai would be up on the mountain right now.

It was one of those misty, moist days that doesn't know if it wants to rain or not. The mountains lurked hidden in the mist. After a few yards on the track Evan was swallowed up into his own private world. This was how he liked it. Half an hour on his own like this and things usually began to make sense. He headed up the Pig Track, the steeper of the two routes, then struck off on a side path, climbing quickly above the lake on the narrow trail that led to the top of Crib Goch. The mist had shrouded the land in silence. No birds chirped. No insects buzzed. The wind wasn't even sighing through the rocks. Even his footsteps on the springy turf sounded muffled.

He was halfway up the slope when he heard footsteps above him. He froze, feeling the back of his neck prickle. This wasn't the sort of day you'd expect to find too many people on the mountain. If there really was a madman up here, then now wasn't the best of times to meet him. He stepped off the path, to the shelter of a large rock, waiting for the person to come past. The footsteps were light and moving fast. Then gradually a strange billowy shape emerged from the mist, with what looked like wings flying out behind it. Evan blinked and stared harder, his heart beating fast as he tried to decide what he was seeing.

Then the mist swirled and cleared for a moment and a smile lit up his face. It was Bronwen and she was wearing a big cloak that flew out behind her as she hurried.

"Bronwen!" He stepped out from behind his rock.

He had forgotten that she had no idea of his presence. She gasped and stepped back, terrified.

"It's only me, Evan," he said, grabbing her arm before she could fall down the slope. "Sorry if I scared you."

"You certainly did," she said, still breathing heavily. "I thought my heart was going to leap out of my chest for a moment there. All this talk of climbers falling mysteriously to their deaths and of Daft Dai being seen again. Suddenly I got scared."

"What were you doing up here?" Evan asked her.

"Looking for the first Snowdon lilies of the season," she said. "They're so rare now and the wretched tourists pick them even though they're a protected species. They call this a national park and then they can't afford to pay enough rangers to police it. It wasn't misty when I started out. I had no idea the mist could come down so quickly."

"Oh, yes," Evan said. "I've known it to come down in literally a few seconds."

"What are you doing up here yourself?" she asked. There was a hint of uneasiness in her voice.

"I often come up here to think," Evan said.

"Were you heading for Crib Goch?" she asked, knowing where the path led.

"Not in this weather, thank you," Evan said, chuckling. "I know these mountains pretty well, but I wouldn't cross Crib Goch in the mist, unless I really had to. One foot wrong and it's a thousand feet of nothing."

"I've never been up there yet, but I hear it's very alarming," she said.

"There's nothing to it in fine weather," Evan said. "It's at least three feet wide all the way. It's just the thought of that drop on either side that makes people lose their nerve. I'll take you up there one fine day if you like."

"That wasn't where those men fell, was it?" she asked, shivering.

"No, that was over on the other side, up above the old mine workings around Glaslyn. Not a spot you see too many climbers."

"You still think there was something suspicious about those deaths?" she asked.

"I'm sure of it," Evan said. He looked around. "The mist is getting worse. I'll come down with you, so that you don't miss the path."

"I'll be fine," she said. "Don't let me keep you from your hike."

"I don't think I'll bother to go further up today," Evan said. "To tell you the truth, I'd welcome the chance to talk to someone. I'm in a bit of a quandary about where to go next."

"I'm a good listener," Bronwen said as she began to follow him down the trail. "Do you think their deaths were suspicious?"

"It's all a question of connections," Evan said. "I'm a great believer in connections."

"What do you mean?"

"I suppose it's being outside a lot, up here in the mountains," Evan said. "If you look at nature, nothing happens in isolation. Every plant, every insect, is part of a chain. We're all linked together from the smallest spider on up. The first thing I always do when I have to tackle a crime, is to look for the connections. Well, I've looked here and I've come up with some pretty good ones."

He took her elbow to help her down a steep part. She smiled at him. The mist was sitting like diamonds on her eyelashes. Evan thought he'd never seen her looking so pretty and he lost his train of thought for a moment.

"Now, Sergeant Watkins," he said, firmly bringing his mind back to the matter in hand, "he thinks we're dealing with a madman. He's got his men out looking for Daft Dai. I must admit that theory sounded pretty good to me at first. But now I'm not so sure it's him we want."

"Why not?" She looked back as she went ahead of him.

"Because I can almost guarantee that those men knew each other and that they were here for a reason," Evan said. "I don't want to say too much until I've checked my facts, but that's the hunch I'm going on."

"And how will you check your facts?"

"Ah, that's the problem I'm up against," Evan said. "I believe they were in the army together, at the same base at the same time. But the army isn't going to tell me anything without an official request."

"And you can't get one?"

"The sergeant's looking for Daft Dai. He's more or less told me that I'm a village copper and I shouldn't be sticking my nose in where it's not wanted. And he's got the murder of this little girl down in Caernarfon on his hands too."

"I know all about that," Bronwen said, shivering. "I've warned my kids at school not to wander off alone until this man is caught. She was about the same age as the girls in my top class."

"We'll catch the bastard," Evan muttered. "It's only a matter of time."

"I just pray he doesn't strike again before they do catch him," Bronwen said. "It's not a question of prudence and lying low. That type of man can't help himself."

"They've got everyone at headquarters working on it around the clock," Evan said. "That's one of the reasons Sergeant Watkins would love to call the climbers' deaths an accident or the work of a madman. Then he could close this case and get on with the important stuff."

"You say you think they knew each other and they were there for a reason," Bronwen said, pausing on a level stretch of path to look back at Evan. "Are you saying they were brought there to be killed?"

"I hadn't thought of it like that," Evan admitted.

"Why?" Bronwen asked.

Evan shrugged. "I suppose I'll know more when I can find out who was invited and who wrote the invitation."

Bronwen shook her head so that the diamond drops flew off her hair. "You'd need a pretty strong motive to lure two men up a mountain and then kill them," she said.

"Either that or you'd need to be crazy," Evan agreed. "It's just possible that someone like Daft Dai did manage to sneak up behind both of them and push them over separate cliffs, but there are too many coincidences. If they were up a there as a memorial to another tragic death, that has to have something to do with it."

"So where do you go from here?" Bronwen asked.

"I don't think I have an alternative," Evan said. "If I want to find out more from the army, I'll have to drive over to the base in Yorkshire myself."

"That's a long drive," Bronwen said. "Will they let you go?"

Evan grinned. "I thought I might just not tell anyone. The village can do without me for a day and my phone system will put anyone who calls through to HQ if there's an emergency."

"Do you think you'd get in trouble if they found out?"

"Probably," Evan said. "Unless I solved the case for them."

"What could they do to you?" Bronwen looked worried. "I wouldn't want you to lose your job."

"I don't think it would come to that," Evan said sounding more convinced than he really felt. "The very worst they could do would be to give me a stern reprimand and dock me a day's pay."

"You could always tell them you were on the mountain, looking for Daft Dai," Bronwen suggested. "You'd be incommunicado up there, wouldn't you?"

"I don't know, Bronwen," Evan said. "I'm a straightforward kind of chap. I never did like telling lies, even if they were for a good reason."

Bronwen smiled to herself as if he'd given the right answer in a quiz.

"I just hope my old car will hold up that far," Evan said. "I'd have to go unofficially and not wear my uniform and just hope that I can get people to talk to me out of the goodness of their hearts."

"I'm sure your boyish charm will win through," she said, giving him a challenging smile. "It usually does."

She was delighted to see that he blushed.

The Everest Inn loomed out of the mist ahead of them.

Evan found himself thinking about Major Anderson. He hadn't heard a peep out of him since they'd viewed the body on Monday. Maybe the major thought his duty was done now. Then it crossed Evan's mind that the major was an ex-army man too. It might have been worth finding out if Major Anderson had also been at Caterick base in 1990. He was, after all, the one who had known first that Tommy Hatcher was missing. Something had struck Evan as odd about that at the time. Surely busy hotel managers only noticed their guests were missing if they hadn't slept in their beds, didn't they? And yet it was still light when the major had sounded the alarm.

Bronwen touched his arm.

"I'd better be getting back to correcting my science tests," she said.

"Oh, yes. Of course." Evan looked down at her. She looked just right, somehow, standing there in her red cape with the mist swirling about her, like a heroine from an old novel. He had an absurd desire to take her into his arms, and told himself sternly that this was neither the time or the place. "And I better be getting back to work too," he added. "I should get out the road map and study the best route for tomorrow. I don't fancy driving all those congested roads through Manchester."

Bronwen put her hand on his sleeve. "Take care of yourself, won't you, Evan," she said. "If someone really has pushed two men to their deaths, he or she wouldn't hesitate to do it a third time. I don't want you getting yourself into something you can't handle alone."

"Don't worry about me," Evan said. "I can take care of myself pretty well. And don't you go wandering up mountains alone again in the mist, Bronwen Price."

"I can take care of myself too, Evan Evans." She flashed

him a smile. "Let me know if you find anything in Yorkshire, won't you?"

"I will," he said. He watched her go ahead of him until she was safely to the schoolhouse door before he hurried down the path to the police station.

The figure who had perched unseen among the rocks gradually straightened up and stretched cramped legs. The conversation had been most interesting. It paid to hang around and listen. Eventually someone would give the right piece of information. The figure turned and took off up the tortuous track with the easy grace of a wild animal. The mountain watched and waited.

Chapter 9

Evan slipped out of the house at six o'clock the next morning. If he'd told Mrs. Williams he had a long drive ahead of him, she would have had eggs, bacon, and possibly kippers on the table waiting for him. Evan pictured kippers lying on a plate in the dawn's early light and decided to creep out unnoticed.

It was a clear, fresh morning and the mountains stood out as if they had been etched against the sky. Again Evan was breathtaken by their loveliness. The sight of them made him want to forget about his expedition and put in an early morning hike, but then he remembered those two battered bodies lying broken on the rocks. It didn't seem right that something so lovely could also be so deadly. They had come here unsuspecting, out of compassion for a friend only to meet the same fate. Evan owed it to them to find out the truth and let them rest in peace.

He put his foot to the floorboards as he picked up the A55, heading east for the big cities of Lancashire and Yorkshire, praying that the ten-year-old car would make the trip without breaking down. His early start enabled him to clear Manchester before the rush hour and the motorway whisked him past the worst of Leeds. It was just before ten when he pulled up outside the main gate of Caterick army base.

A gloomy-looking spot if ever he'd seen one, he thought, his eye travelling over the rows of barracks with the bleak moors as backdrop. He could have understood it better if a soldier had been lost and frozen to death in this setting. Why did they have to go all the way over to Wales to do it?

The guard at the main gate was no more helpful than the phone operator had been. He was sorry, he said, but he couldn't let Evan into the base without a pass.

"Look, mate, I've driven all this way," Evan said. Usually he didn't have trouble with people, only those who felt themselves puffed up with authority. He pulled out his badge. "North Wales police. We're trying to solve a murder case—"

"What seems to be the problem, sergeant?" A crisp, upper-class voice demanded. Evan turned to see a young officer approaching.

"He says he's a policeman, sir," the gatekeeper said, "but I don't rightly know who to direct him to."

The officer held out his hand. "Lieutenant Pitcher. How can I help you?"

Evan shook the hand that was offered. "Evans, North Wales police," he said. "I'm here looking into a couple of suspicious deaths. We think that both of the men might have been stationed at this base."

"Two of our men killed? We haven't heard anything about it."

"Not stationed here now," Evan said, hoping the man

90

wasn't going to be too slow on the uptake. "The only connection between them seems to be that they were mates in the army once."

"And you think that might have had something to do with their deaths?"

Evan nodded encouragingly. "Their deaths might have been linked to an earlier incident. There was a soldier from this base who died during a survival training exercise on Mount Snowdon about six years ago."

The friendly expression faded from the man's face. "I don't think you'll find anybody here who wants to bring that up again," he said. "It was before my time, but there was an awful fuss, I gather. We had the top brass asking questions and quite a few stripes got ripped off. There are still hard feelings."

"I don't really want to bring it up again," Evan said. "I just need to find out if there was any connection between the two men that died on the mountain last Sunday and the man who died six years ago. There is some evidence that they used to be mates."

"And if they were?" the lieutenant asked.

"Then their deaths have to be linked somehow," Evan said. "For two of them to die in the same place, at the same time of year as the first tragedy would be too much of a coincidence."

The lieutenant nodded. "Yes, I see your point," he said. "I'm not sure what I can do to help you. Any official enquiry would have to be made to Major Harrison, of course."

"You could be a lot of help to me if we could just take a peek at the records and confirm that they were here at the same time," Evan said. "That wouldn't need to go via Major Harrison, would it?"

"I suppose that would be easy enough," the lieutenant

said. "We've got it all on computers now. Ten years behind the outside world, of course, but the army's finally catching up. Let's go and see what we can do, shall we?"

It only took a few minutes in a clerk's office and there were the names on the screen. Hatcher, Thomas, private. Intake 137F, spring 1990. Potts, Stewart, private. Intake 137F. Bartholomew, Danny, private. Intake 137F.

"They all got here at the same time," Evan commented. "That's a start, isn't it?"

"And what now?" Lieutenant Pitcher asked. He looked quite excited about the chance to join in solving the murders.

"Is it possible that anyone here might remember them?" Evan asked. "If they were mates, then there had to be another mate in the picture—the one who sent the card. The one who's still alive."

"The card?" Lieutenant Pitcher asked.

"A postcard was sent to Tommy Hatcher inviting him to a memorial for Danny up on the mountain, on the anniversary of the day he died. Someone had to have sent that postcard."

"Yes, I see what you mean," Lieutenant Pitcher said. "There is Sergeant Spinks. He's been here for ever. All the new recruits get him at some stage and God, do they hate him. His name is Abraham Spinks and they call him Bad Ham Stinks." He grinned boyishly. Evan decided he probably wasn't much over twenty and tried to picture himself with authority over a lot of men at that age. Maybe an equally young officer was in charge of Danny Bartholemew that night on the mountain and gave him the wrong orders which resulted in his getting lost . . .

At first glance Evan thought that he'd get nothing out of Sergeant Spinks. The man had an impassive face, so weather-worn that it looked as if it was made of old leather.

"Yeah, I remember the incident all right," he said. "Stupid bugger lost his pack. What's the first thing we tell them? Hang onto your pack!"

Evan wondered if his were some of the stripes that got ripped off as a result of the enquiry.

"You remember Danny Bartholomew then?" Evan asked. "Can you tell me anything about him? Would you say he was the sort of soldier who would lose his way and his pack?"

The old sergeant stared out across the parade ground, then shook his head. "Not really," he said. "I remember that bunch in hut 29. Cheeky buggers, all of them, but not stupid like some of the blokes we get. No, I remember being surprised when I heard. Potts—I wouldn't have put it past him. He never had an inspection he passed first time, always forgetting something. But not Bartholemew. He tried hard. I always thought he was one of the ones who was going to make a soldier some day."

"You remember Potts then?" Evan asked, trying to keep the excitement from his voice. "He was one of Danny's mates?"

The sergeant stared out across the parade ground again. "Potts, Bartholemew, Hatcher, and Marshall—that was it. I always used to catch them after lights out. I bet they made good husbands—they certainly learned how to peel enough spuds here." The leather face cracked into a grin.

"Marshall?" Evan asked. "Remember his first name or anything about him?"

But the sergeant shook his head. "He was Marshall to me. That's all I remember."

"Thanks for your help," Evan said, shaking Lieutenant Pitcher's hand as they walked back to the main gate.

"I'm sorry we couldn't find out any more for you," Lieutenant Pitcher said. "I'm afraid you'll have to send in an official request if you want to look at their army records and get current addresses."

"At least I've got something to go on now, haven't I?" Evan said. "At least I've proved they were all friends. That's a good start."

As he drove back to Wales, he tried to put his thoughts in order. Marshall was the missing link. Now that he had something definite to go on, he could ask Sergeant Watkins to officially request Marshall's army records and they could find out his address. Then he'd know if Marshall was the one who sent the postcard and if he was on the mountain that day.

The clear morning had turned into a gray afternoon as Evan arrived back in Llanfair at four o'clock. Clouds hung low over the mountains, giving the impression that Llanfair existed in complete isolation, cut off from the outside world. A cold wind swirled fingers of mist down the mountainsides, and Evan drew his jacket around him as he headed for the police station door. As he turned the key in the lock, he suddenly had the feeling that someone was watching him. He looked around but saw nobody. I'm turning into a nervous old lady, he told himself.

There was no message light flashing on his answering machine and he let out a sigh of relief as he sat at his desk. He looked up and started as a shadow fell across him.

"Its' only me," Betsy's voice said. "Keep your hair on, Evan Evans."

"Oh, Betsy. I didn't hear you come in," Evan said. "you made me jump."

"They say I'm very light on my feet," Betsy said, smiling

down at him. "That's why you didn't hear me coming. And speaking of being light on my feet, I was wondering about the dance on Saturday."

"Saturday?" Evan's mind was momentarily blank. He wondered if he had recently been drunk enough to have promised to take Betsy dancing.

"You know, the teen dance at the hall? I heard you were going to be a chaperon."

"Oh, that's right," Evan said. "So much has happened this week that it completely slipped my mind."

"Pity I've already turned twenty, isn't it?" Betsy said, her eyes teasing him. "Or you'd have finally had to dance with me. Of course, they might still need chaperons, if Harry would let me off early on Saturday night." She paused and left the sentence unfinished.

Evan swallowed hard and wondered what important criminal event could come up on Saturday that would take him far away from the village hall. The thought of dancing with Betsy, her voluptuous body pressed against his, was too disturbing.

She perched herself on the edge of his desk. "So where have you been gone all day?" she asked. "There was a strange police car up here, looking for you."

Evan's heart sank. "Looking for me? Did they say why?"

"No. It wasn't me they asked. Maybe it had to do with those two poor men on the mountain." Evan decided that Betsy might look like the typical dumb blonde, but she was sharp enough when she wanted to be. "Charlie was talking about it in the pub at lunchtime today," she went on. "He said something about those men being up on the mountain for a memorial."

Evan nodded. "Something like that."

Betsy made a face. "Funny old place to hold a memorial, wouldn't you say? If it was me, I'd hold it in the pub, not up on a windy mountain."

"A girl after my own heart," Evan said and instantly wished he had chosen his words more carefully. Betsy was too eager to find encouragement in any innocuous comment. "If ever you're in charge of my wake," he went on hurriedly, "make sure it's held at the Red Dragon. Tell Harry free drinks all around."

Betsy looked alarmed. "You're not thinking of dying just yet, are you Evan Evans? Not when there's so many people who need you."

As she talked she slipped off the corner of the desk and inched herself closer to him until she had eased herself onto the arm of his chair. "People who are counting on your being around here for a long while yet." Her hand crept along his shoulder.

A sudden wind sent the papers on his desk swirling and Evan looked up to see Bronwen standing in the doorway. She was wearing a red parka and the wind had given her rosy cheeks to match it. Her normally tidy braid was loose, and stray curls framed her face as it quickly changed from happiness to a stony mask.

"Oh, sorry, I see you're occupied," she said, her voice clipped. "I just stopped by to see how your mission went. I can come back later."

She made a rapid exit.

"Bronwen, wait," Evan called, trying to get up without pitching Betsy to the floor. But she had gone.

"She doesn't like it that we're such good friends," Betsy said, giving Evan's shoulder a little squeeze as she got up. "Well, I should be getting on my way too, Evan Evans. See

96

you at the dance on Saturday then. Save a slow dance for me, won't you?"

"Damn," Evan muttered as she closed the door behind her.

Almost immediately the phone rang. "Where the hell were you all bloody day?" Sergeant Watkins demanded. "There was a breaking and entering in your village and nobody knew where you were. We had to send a car from HQ. They asked me if you were on assignment for me." He paused. "I saved your damned skin and said we'd had a report that Daft Dai might have been seen up on the mountain."

"Thanks, sarge," Evan said. "What was the breaking and entering about?"

"A Mrs. Powell-Jones," Sergeant Watkins said. "She wasn't very helpful to our blokes. She said she wanted you to handle it but she couldn't reach you."

Evan sighed. "I wonder what it was this time? Stolen brussels sprouts?"

"She's one of those old biddies who make trouble, is she?"

"You can say that again," Evan said. "I suppose I'll have to go up and see what she wants. Look, sarge, I really appreciate the way you covered for me."

"Just out of curiosity, where were you?" Sergeant Watkins said. "Was it official business or were you just playing hookey?"

"Oh it was business all right," Evan said. "Look, sarge, I think I might have found an interesting line of enquiry on our two mountain murders. I went to Yorkshire and—"

"Hold on a minute, Evans," Sergeant Watkins voice became hard. "You went to Yorkshire? Who gave you permission to do that?"

"Nobody but—"

"Let's get one thing straight. If those two deaths weren't

accidents—and I'm prepared to give you the benefit of the doubt on that—then there's only one suspect we're pursuing and our men are out looking for him right now. So stop playing detective, okay?"

"Okay, but sarge—" Evan began when Watkins cut him off.

"Listen here, Evans. You're a village policeman, not bloody Inspector Morse. If I find you poking your nose in where it's not wanted and going off on hare-brained schemes of your own again, I'll report you to your chief. Do I make myself clear?"

"Perfectly clear, sarge," Evan said. "And I promise I'll stop interfering if you'd just do me one favor and have the War Office look up an army record for me."

"The War Office? You can go up on the mountains and find Daft Dai for us if it makes you happy, but that's it. My DCI is not giving anyone time to breathe until we've brought in Lou Walters and solved the little girl's murder. That's all I care about right now."

"Any closer to finding him?"

"We know he's been seen in the area," Watkins said. "We suspect his mother knows where he is, but she's not saying. These mothers make me sick. Their sons might be Hitler and the devil rolled into one, but they won't think of turning them in. You'll be getting a description. We're sending them out to all the small stations, just in case he's staying away from the towns."

"Right-o, sarge. I'll keep my eyes open then," Evan said.

"I'd give anything to catch that bastard, Evans," Sergeant Watkins muttered. There was a click as he put down the phone.

Evan sat there, staring at the Beautyspots of Wales calendar on his wall. So Sergeant Watkins wasn't going to be any help in getting Marshall's address. Evan wondered how he could hope to find it himself, now that he'd been forbidden to pursue the case any further. He wondered what the punishment might be in a situation like this. Surely they wouldn't fire him for being overzealous? The worst they could give him would be a stern warning and that as a risk he was willing to take, if it solved a couple of murders.

Marshall. He wrote the word on his memo pad. There were a lot of Marshall's in the British Isles. Maybe if he wrote to the War Office on official police stationary? He opened the file which now contained the photo of Stewart Potts and his wife and printouts of the articles on Danny Bartholemew's death. It might be worth calling Greta Potts, on the off-chance that she might remember someone called Marshall or might be able to find his address among Stew's possessions.

But first he had another assignment: Mrs. Powell-Jones would not wait another minute for justice.

Chapter 10

Evan put on his uniform jacket and cap. Then walked briskly up the village street toward the Powell-Jones residence, his pace hardly a reflection of his anticipation, only a desire to get this over with.

As he approached the school grounds, he caught a glimpse of Bronwen crossing the school yard.

"Bronwen!" he called, but she only walked faster.

Evan broke into a run and caught her halfway across the netball court. "Hold on a minute. What's the rush?"

"I've got math tests I should be correcting," Bronwen said, her face impassive but her cheeks flushed pink.

"Look, Bronwen, I just wanted to explain," Evan said.

"You don't have to explain to me," Bronwen said. "What you do with your own time is up to you, Evan Evans."

"It wasn't how it looked at all," Evan said miserably. "Betsy just popped in to talk to me about a spot of volunteer work I'm doing."

"Volunteering to do what exactly?" Bronwen asked, giving him a look that was half-amused, half-challenging.

"Help out with the youth group dance on Saturday, if you really want to know. Betsy was just checking that I was still on."

"And were you still on?"

Evan cursed his choice of words again. That was the problem of growing up with Welsh as his number-one language. English had a habit of letting him down.

"It was just a harmless little discussion, that's all," Evan said.

"And does she always do her discussing sitting on someone's knee with her arm around their neck?" Bronwen asked defiantly.

"She was sitting on the arm of my chair and I didn't encourage her, if that's what you're thinking."

"I noticed you weren't struggling too hard either," Bronwen said. "Let's just forget it, shall we? I've got a million things I should be doing."

With that she hurried into the school and shut the door behind her firmly before Evan could do anything. He turned and sighed as he walked back to the road. The problem was that he had never crossed that line with Bronwen. He had no claim on her. She wasn't his girlfriend. He hadn't been sure that he wanted to cross it. He had told himself that she was a little too serious and intense for him. He wanted a girl with more warmth and feeling. But now, as he recalled her flushed cheeks and her eyes flashing angry fire at him, he had to wonder if there wasn't more feeling than he'd imagined hidden under that cool exterior.

He put on a resolute face and walked briskly up to Mrs. Powell-Jones' house.

"Finally!" Mrs. Powell-Jones exclaimed as she opened the

front door. "I have been most distressed all day, Constable Evans. Most distressed. Nobody knew where you were at your headquarters. I find that most strange."

"I'm in the middle of a case, Mrs. Powell-Jones," Evan said. "I can't be at the police station all day. Weren't the men from HQ able to help you out?"

"I sent them away again. I told you, I don't want strangers interfering in this matter," Mrs. Powell-Jones said. "It is most delicate and I do feel for poor Mr. Parry Davies. It must be difficult enough for him to live with such a wife."

"And what do you suspect she's done now?"

"Suspect?" Mrs. Powell-Jones demanded. "I know."

"You saw her? You caught her in the act?"

"Not exactly, but as good as. She came over here this morning, constable. She said she wanted to see what food my ladies were bringing to the teen dance on Saturday. Of course I realize now that that was only an excuse. She knows we always bring the cheese and pickle sandwiches and the fairy cakes. Anyway, it was about an hour after she had gone that I noticed it was missing."

"What was missing?" Evan asked.

"My apple pie," she said.

"Apple pie?"

"Yes, I'd just baked it and I had it on the kitchen window sill, cooling. The window was open. When I came back into the kitchen around noon, the pie had gone."

"Excuse me for asking, but what possible interest could Mrs. Parry Davies have had in your pie?" Evan asked.

"It's simple, man. She's developed this deep-seated jealousy. She knows her pastry is inferior to mine. When she passed my window on her way out, she couldn't resist the temptation. She's probably whisked it home and served it up to poor Mr.

Parry Davies as her own. If only you'd been here when I first called, you could probably have caught her with a forkful of the evidence going to her mouth. Now I'm afraid we're too late."

"I'm sorry about your pie, Mrs. Powell-Jones," Evan said. "But there's really not much I can do. And I am very busy . . ."

"Of course there's something you can do," she said. "If you had any police training or skill at all, you'd be able to go over there and get her to confess."

"I'm sorry, but they don't let us use the rack or the thumb screws any more," Evan said. "I could shut her in a dungeon down at Caernarfon Castle, if you'd like."

"Don't be facetious, young man," Mrs. Powell-Jones snapped. "If it were left to me, I should have no trouble extracting a confession from her. I had no trouble at all getting the Boy Scouts to own up when they had sneaked into my back garden and stolen my apples. One look from me and they burst into tears."

Evan wasn't surprised. Mrs. Powell-Jones had a similar effect on him.

"Before you go making any more accusations, I think you should know that it's possible there is a Peeping Tom in the area," Evan said. "A man they used to call Daft Dai."

"Daft Dai? He's around again? I thought they put him away years ago."

"Well, now it seems they've let him out," Evan said. "It's possible he's come back to the area. So I'd advise you to keep your windows shut and pull your curtains until we find out more."

"Thank you, constable. I will." For the first time, Mrs. Powell-Jones sounded almost human. "But that doesn't mean that Mrs. Parry Davies is not my number-one suspect," she added. "I shall still be keeping a close eye on her, and so should you, Constable Evans."

As Evan came out of the Powell-Jones house, he noticed that the billboards outside the two chapels had been changed. The Powell-Jones billboard now read, "Thou shalt not steal," and the board opposite stated, "Let him who is without sin cast the first stone."

They didn't waste a minute, Evan thought, smiling.

He found himself picturing the two feuding ministers and their wives, Bibles always at the ready, peering out of their windows to see if another text had gone up on the opposite billboard.

A loud shout broke his reverie. He looked up to see two people running down the path above the Everest Inn. They were dressed in hiking gear and carried backpacks. Evan hurried to meet them. As he got closer, he saw that they were a young couple, their faces red with effort.

"Oh, thank heavens, constable," the young man gasped. "We were wondering where we'd locate the closest police station."

"Got a problem, have you?" Evan asked.

"There's a man, up on the mountain!" the girl gasped.

"Dead?"

"No, not dead. Very much alive," the man said. "He grabbed Fiona."

Evan turned to look at the girl who now looked more animated than scared. "It was horrible," she said. "Brian was trying a spot of climbing alone, so I sat on a rock, watching him. Suddenly this man appeared out of nowhere and started shouting at me. He told me to get off the mountain right now or the wrath of God would strike me down. He said he was God's messenger, the keeper of the mountain, and he didn't want foreigners defiling sacred soil."

"Did he harm you in any way?"

"He grabbed me and shook me," she said, shuddering at the memory. "I think he might have thrown me over the edge, but I screamed. Brian heard and came clambering back up to save me. He was awfully brave," she added, smiling up at her hero.

"What happened to the man?" Evan asked.

"He ran off when Brian yelled at him. We didn't see where he went. We thought we should come straight down and find someone to report this to."

"You did the right thing to find me," Evan said. "We've got a bulletin out looking for this chap. If you'll come with me down to the station, I'll get a full report and description of the man, and your names and addresses, if I may. We might need you as witnesses."

"So the police know about him then?"

"Oh, yes," Evan said. "He's wanted for questioning right now, so you've done us a big favor by finding him."

"Is he . . . really dangerous?" Fiona asked, turning large, scared eyes on Evan.

"He hasn't been, up to now." Evan didn't want to give her unnecessary nightmares. "But we can't have him going around scaring people, can we? You give me a good description then I'll get on to HQ. Hopefully we'll have him safely in custody by the end of the day."

"Nice work, Evans," Detective Sergeant Watkins said as they met down at headquarters in Caernarfon. "My chief wants me to compliment you and your lads on the efficient way you apprehended the suspect."

"Thanks, sarge," Evans said. "It wasn't very hard, actually. The blokes I took with me up the mountain recognized him right away. He was sitting on a rock eating a sandwich. I went up to him and said 'Are you Dai?' and he said he was. When I asked him to come with me, he came, meek as a lamb."

"Did he say anything useful?" Watkins asked.

"I didn't attempt to question him," Evan said. "I didn't think that was my job."

"Quite right," Sergeant Watkins said. "We've got him in holding room 2. He's been read his rights. You want to come with me while I question him? I might need an interpreter," he added. "My Welsh isn't that good."

The man known as Daft Dai was sitting at the table with a cup of tea in front of him. He was skinny, underfed, and inoffensive-looking, with thinning hair and thick-lensed glasses. He was dressed in a mismatched series of oddments so that he looked like a walking rag bag. He looked up and smiled when Sergeant Watkins and Evans came into the room. He seemed quite comfortable and not in the least anxious as they sat down opposite him.

"Dai, what's this we've been hearing about you annoying people up on the mountain again?" Sergeant Watkins began amiably.

"It was more of those foreigners," Dai said. "I told them to stay away but they won't listen, will they? They keep coming back."

Sergeant Watkins turned to his own constable who was standing on guard behind Dai. "Was he carrying a weapon?"

"Only a pocket knife," the sergeant said.

"What did you want a knife for, Dai?" Sergeant Watkins asked.

"To cut up my orange," Dai answered, making Evan smile to himself.

"Dai, I'm going to ask you another question. I want you to tell the truth," Sergeant Watkins said gently. "A few days ago two men were killed up on the mountain. We don't think they just slipped and fell. We think somebody might have pushed them. Can you tell us anything about that, Dai?"

There was silence in the room. Dai was staring at his tea cup.

"Did you push those men, Dai?" Sergeant Watkins asked. "Better to tell the truth and get it off your chest, isn't it?"

Dai swallowed hard. "I did it," he said. "I killed them. The mountain told me to."

Chapter 11

"Thank heavens for that," Sergeant Watkins said as Evan prepared to drive back to Llanfair later that afternoon. "I'd say that all ended very satisfactorily." He patted Evan on the back with a big hearty thump. "Thanks to you and your sharp eyes. I'd have let it go as two accidents. You knew better, didn't you? And then you go and catch the blighter for us."

Evan cringed with embarrassment but managed a smile. He hated being praised more than anything. "Just a bit of luck really, sarge," he said. "If those two hikers hadn't been so quick to report him . . ."

"Anyhow, we've got a killer safely put away for life this time, and that's all that matters," Sergeant Watkins said. "He'll be back in the loony bin where he belongs, and probably very happy to be there again."

Evan nodded.

"You can tell that nice kid Fiona how lucky she is to be

alive," Sergeant Watkins went on. "Dai might have shoved her over a cliff too."

Sergeant Watkins went on talking and Evan went on smiling, but he couldn't stop the uneasy feelings that were creeping into the back of his brain. He was glad it had ended so easily and with nobody else getting hurt, but it didn't seem right somehow. It was too simple. Just how had a meek, frail-looking little man like Dai managed to push two hefty blokes over cliffs? One of them he could understand, but two? Especially if they had been together. And Dai hadn't been any more help. When asked for details, he had given them several fanciful tales about angels sweeping the men off rocks with their wings or the wrath of God smiting them with lightning strikes.

"I'm glad we've got those two kids as witnesses," Evan said. "Just in case Dai changes his mind and gets a do-gooding lawyer who decides to make him plead not guilty."

Sergeant Watkins nodded. "They make it a pretty watertight case. I can't see Dai wriggling out of this one."

"You don't think he could have had anything to do with the other murder, do you, sarge?" Evan asked cautiously. "He is loony enough after all. It would take a deranged man to do what he did to that little girl."

"I did sort of mention it to him," Sergeant Watkins said. "And he categorically denied it. He looked shocked and kept on saying that he loves little kids, so I'm inclined to believe him. And he has no record of bothering children in any way."

"Pity," Evan said. "It would be nice to sew them both up at the same time."

"It would have been bloody marvelous," Sergeant Watkins said. "But at least we can devote all our energy to finding the little girl's killer now, thanks to you and your quick thinking. This will go down on your permanent record, you know. And if you ever wanted to transfer back to the criminal investigation side . . ."

"No thanks, sarge. In spite of what you think, I'm quite happy where I am right now," said Evan. "I've had enough excitement in the last few days to keep me going for a while."

Sergeant Watkins slapped Evan on the back again. "Come on, I owe you a beer, don't I?"

"Save it for later, sarge," Evan said, the uneasiness creeping back. "Let's wait until he's officially pleaded guilty and been sentenced." He noticed Sergeant Watkins' querying glance. "I like to see things wrapped up nice and neat, see?"

On the way home Evan hoped that during the next round of questioning, Dai might also confess to being Mrs. Powell-Jones' Peeping Tom. Evan played the scene through in his head, telling her that she need not worry any longer. He had solved her problems. She'd never again be bothered by the man who stole her apple pie and stepped on her flower beds. He might even insist that she went and apologized to Mrs. Parry Davies. That would be worth seeing!

On Friday morning Evan got up to find a hero's breakfast waiting for him.

"Evans-the-Meat sent over some of his best pork sausages," said Mrs. Williams as Evan sat down to two rashers of bacon, two fried eggs, fried bread crisped golden in the bacon fat, fried tomatoes, mushrooms, and two fat sausages—browned nicely on the outsides and splitting their skins to reveal their juicy interior.

"This is a very big breakfast for a weekday, Mrs. Williams," he protested, halfheartedly, the tempting smell of bacon and sausage already playing havoc with his taste buds.

"Nonsense. You deserve it. You need your strength if you

will go chasing mad men up mountains." She smiled at him fondly. "They're saying you were a real hero, the way you managed to arrest him—they're saying you went over to him and clapped the handcuffs on him, cool as a cucumber."

"It really wasn't hard, Mrs. Williams," Evan said, feeling hot around the collar again.

"That's not what I'm hearing," Mrs. Williams said. Evan knew what had happened. Those who had gone with Evan up the mountain to help him capture Daft Dai had told those who stayed behind all about it in the pub, embellishing the drama and danger with each telling. By now it probably sounded like an episode from a BBC police drama.

"I called my daughter last night and she told Sharon," Mrs. Williams confided. "And do you know what Sharon said? She said 'I always knew he was going to be a hero some day!' I told my daughter it's a pity that Sharon can't get over here for the dance tomorrow night."

"It's for the teens, Mrs. Williams," Evan said quickly, happy to remember proud grandma's account of Sharon's twenty-first. "Sharon's not a teen any longer and I'm only a chaperon."

"Sharon could help you with your chaperoning. She's ever so good with the little kiddies, you know. She's going to make a lovely mum some day . . . and maybe you two could sneak a little dance together. She dances lovely—like a little fairy on her feet, she is."

A vision of Sharon swam into Evan's head. Definitely a well-built girl who took after her grandma around the hips. He couldn't imagine her wafting around like a fairy. But he could imagine Betsy's face if she saw him dancing with Sharon. Those two would probably be locked in mortal combat by the end of the evening, he decided.

"I'll be too busy to think of dancing, Mrs. Williams," he said quickly. "I heard some of those boys might be trying to smuggle alcohol into the dance. I'm going to have my hands full enough, watching them."

Hastily he tucked into the pork sausages before Mrs. Williams could begin her next round of matchmaking.

After breakfast his uniform pants felt decidedly tight around the waist as he began his morning patrol through the village. Checking out the neighborhood on foot was one of the things he liked about being a village policeman. You just didn't get that same feel of a place from the interior of a police car. And now it had been proved—there was less crime when areas were patrolled on foot and policemen built up a rapport with the locals. Evan could have told them that when they experimented with centralization a few years ago and closed down all the local stations in favor of cruising police cars. He was glad they'd gone back to village bobbies again.

It had been raining, but patches of blue peeped out between racing clouds. Llanfair was already awake and busy as Evan came out of Mrs. Williams' cottage. Evans-the-Milk was making deliveries from his van, and the cheerful clatter of milk bottles echoed back from the valley walls. A tractor rumbled past with two black-and-white sheepdogs running on either side of it and a newborn lamb lying across the farmer's lap. Front doors were open as housewives beat mats, shook feather dusters, or polished brass door knockers. The women of Llanfair were fierce rivals over who had the shiniest brass on their front doors.

All the way up the street, Evan was greeted as a hero until his face was hot with embarrassment. He began to think that foot patrols weren't such a great idea after all.

The children in the school yard, waiting for the first bell, rushed across to the fence as he passed.

"Are they going to give you a medal then, Mr. Evans? Did he have a gun? Did he really try to throw Mr. Harris down the mountain? Did you have to fight him?"

Evan smiled good-naturedly.

"I saw him, creeping around one night," little Meryl Hopkins, Charlie's granddaughter, exclaimed in her high, musical voice.

"You never did!" The bigger boys looked at her with scorn.

"I did too," Meryl insisted. "I looked out of my window and I saw him, creeping around. Very big and scary looking he was! Ugly and creeping like a great monster."

"Get away with you! You're such a liar, Meryl Hopkins," one of the children said, laughing, and pretty soon they were all teasing her so that she ran away.

Evan continued on up the street, but he wasn't smiling. He paused to look at the Hopkins' cottage. Meryl's window would look straight into the Powell-Jones' backyard. So maybe she had been telling the truth after all. And even a skinny little bloke like Dai would seem scary to a child in the shadowy moonlight.

Evan was tempted to stop by and tell Mrs. Powell-Jones the news, if she hadn't already heard, but he decided against it. Why spoil a lovely day by talking to Mrs. Powell-Jones if he didn't have to?

He got back to his office and had just put the kettle on for a midmorning coffee when his phone rang.

"Is that the police station?" a man's voice asked shakily.

"That's right. Constable Evans speaking."

"Constable Evans, this is Bryan Griffith from the railway in Llanberis."

114

"Oh, right, Mr. Griffith. What can I do for you?"

"It's dreadful, Mr. Evans. Something dreadful's happened," he said. He pronounced it *treadful*, just like Mrs. Williams.

"What is it?"

"Send someone up here quick! They've found another body on the mountain."

Chapter 12

"Damn," Sergeant Watkins muttered as he stepped off the mountain railway at the summit station to find Evan waiting for him. "I thought we'd got this bloody business all squared away. The stupid bastard confessed! You're sure this one's not a real accident?"

"I don't think so, sarge," Evan said grimly. "He's had his throat cut."

"Christ—then maybe this death has nothing to do with the others."

"It's possible," Evan said. "Although three killings in one week—that's a little too much of a coincidence, wouldn't you say?"

"It does seem like it," Sergeant Watkins said. "Oh well, let's take a look at the body."

"Okay, sarge, but watch your footing. It's steep."

Evan led him down a narrow path that zigzagged across the cliff face as it dropped toward the small upper lake, Glaslyn.

"Who found him?" Sergeant Watkins asked.

"A young climber. He saw the blood, trickling down the rock and went to investigate. If the poor bloke hadn't bled so much, we might never have found him. The body's back in a little cave and you don't even notice the entrance until you're right on it."

"Where's the chap who found the body? Did you get his particulars?" Watkins asked, picking his way with great caution as showers of pebbles bounced down from his feet and dropped into the lake below.

"I told him to wait at the snack bar in case you wanted to question him, sarge," Evan said. "He needed a cup of tea anyway. He was as white as a sheet and I don't blame him." He started to clamber across a rocky area of scree and rubble, looking back to make sure Sergeant Watkins was okay.

"This is the old mine workings, sarge. There used to be a copper mine up here. It's my guess that this was a tunnel that partially collapsed."

At first glance Watkins couldn't see the cave. A big slab of rock lay across the entrance. But he saw the trickle of blood, coming out from behind the slab and running over the light gray of the granite below it.

"You didn't touch anything?" he asked Evans.

Evan shook his head. "Don't worry, sarge. I'm not a complete idiot, you know."

"I know, but . . ." Sergeant Watkins began.

"It only took one look to know he was dead. Then I cleared everybody out of this area and called you."

Sergeant Watkins looked back to the two constables he had brought with him. "I want the whole summit area cleared of people, Morgan," he said. "Send them down on the train and don't let anybody else up here until we're done. And get a police cordon around the site."

"And you'll want to stop them coming up the other tracks too," Evan said. "Not everybody takes the train, you know."

"Ah, right," Sergeant Watkins said as if this had never occurred to him before. "You hear that, Morgan? Send down a message to have all the access routes to the summit cordoned off too. Knowing Inspector Hughes, he'll definitely want to take over this case himself, as soon as he gets back—and he's a stickler for everything done by the book." He stepped cautiously across a trickle of water that crossed the path. "He's away today, thank God, gone down to Scotland Yard and going through files on this child killer." He looked at Evan. "So it's up to us at the moment. We have to make sure we get all the details and don't overlook anything. If there's a big rainstorm tonight, it could all be washed away." He looked up at the sky, which had become threatening again.

Evan noticed he had said "us." So he was no longer thought of as the stupid village bobby. At least that was gratifying.

He stood back as Sergeant Watkins crawled gingerly into the cave, then followed him. The bile rose in his throat at the thought of what he was going to find there. It could hardly be described as a cave or a tunnel any longer, just an indent into the cliff, the passage behind it now blocked with boulders from an old collapse. The great slab across the entrance allowed only a thin strip of daylight to enter. Inside the damp mustiness was mixed with the acrid stench of death.

He had been a young man, healthy, fresh-faced, dressed as if he was used to the outdoors with well-worn boots. This had been a real climber, not an amateur from the Everest Inn. He was sitting up, leaning against one of the great boulders that now blocked the passage behind, and he looked, at first glance, as if he was resting. But his eyes were open wide in surprise and there was an ugly red gash, almost from ear to ear.

"Whoever did that had to have a very sharp knife or be very strong," Watkins commented. He looked around. "Pity the floor's solid rock. Not much chance of footprints," he said. "How long do you reckon he's been dead?"

"Not long. The blood was still flowing when I got here."

"Which means the killer is still on the mountain?"

"There are enough ways to get down the mountain without being noticed," Evan said. "He could have taken the train down with everyone else."

"He would have had blood on him, wouldn't he? I'll tell my men to take a good look at everyone as they go down, and I'll notify the local dry cleaners."

"I hardly think he'd be stupid enough take his jacket in to be cleaned around here," Evan said.

"Criminals do the stupidest things sometimes," Sergeant Watkins said. "You'd be surprised. Any sign of the murder weapon?"

"Not that I could see," Evan said. "I looked around a little, but I was careful not to disturb the crime scene. He probably took it with him, wouldn't you say?"

"Plenty of nooks and crannies to hide it here if he wanted to," Sergeant Watkins looked around once more before stepping with great caution out of the cave again. "I won't risk touching anything until forensic gets here," he said. "Who knows, they might pick up a fingerprint or shoeprint that can help us."

"We might know more when we can get at his backpack and find out who he was." Evan gave the dead boy one last glance. The anger he always felt at the senseless loss of young, healthy life made him grit his teeth. Whatever he had done, whoever he had quarreled with, this boy didn't deserve to die.

"Damn and blast," the detective snapped as they headed back up to the summit.

The mountain was now dotted with blue uniforms as policemen fanned out to put up a yellow cordon tape and to shepherd the remaining tourists back to the railway station. An absurd comparison to the sheepdogs he watched every day rounding up the sheep crept into Evan's mind. Life was absurd, he thought.

"So now we're back to square one, eh, Evans?" Sergeant Watkins added.

"Maybe not completely, sarge," Evan said. "If we can find any link between this chap and the other two, then I think we've got something to work with."

"This army business, you mean?"

The last load of tourists was being directed onto the train. Evan noted there was no hysteria, no protests as they lined up and obediently took their seats. That was one good thing about the English, he decided. They were great in a crisis.

"My hare-brained scheme, I believe you called it," Evan couldn't resist saying.

"Maybe it wasn't so bloody hare-brained after all," Sergeant Watkins said. He rubbed his hands together. "It's bloody freezing up here. Let's get a cup of tea while we wait for the lab boys and the photographer."

The tea was strong and tasted as if had been stewing since early morning. Sergeant Watkins made a face, then ladled in several large spoonfuls of sugar.

Evan followed him to one of the concrete benches and they sat down, overlooking the sheer drop down to Glaslyn. Wisps of cloud drifted past them, giving them tantalizing glimpses of blue ocean, blue lakes, and toy villages, before blotting them out again. The wind seemed to blow straight through their clothing.

"Okay, let's have it," Sergeant Watkins said. "Tell me what you've found out so far."

Evan started hesitantly, trying to put things in logical order. Sergeant Watkins got out his notebook and jotted down words from time to time, but didn't interrupt.

"I see," he said at last. "So you're saying that the deaths of the two climbers have to be linked somehow with Danny Bartholemew's death? You think that was murder too?"

"They never found his pack," Evan said. "If you wanted to get rid of someone, leaving him alone on a freezing mountain would be a good way to do it. No one would ever suspect it wasn't an accident."

"So what you're saying," Sergeant Watkins said slowly, "is that we're looking for someone who knew all these men . . . someone who was in the army with them, maybe close to them—had some sort of grudge, maybe?"

"Or needed to shut them up for some reason?" Evan suggested.

"But why wait six years to bump off the other two?" Sergeant Watkins asked.

"Maybe the opportunity wasn't there before," Evan said. "We know that Potts was in Germany. Maybe the killer wanted to wait until all the men were available at the same time." He drained his tea and crushed the paper cup in his hand. "Disgusting stuff," he muttered. Then he sighed. "I don't know, sarge. I've no idea what kind of motive we're looking for, but it does seem as if the answer lies back in the army. Someone sent out an invitation to lure at least one of the men here. We know there was a fourth buddy from hut 29 and he's still alive as far as we know."

122

"What's his name?"

"Marshall," Evan said. "That's all I can tell you about him."

"Army records would have all the details."

"Right," Evan said. He thought it wise not to remind Sergeant Watkins that he had already asked for the army records to be checked on.

"So the first thing to do is to check up on Marshall." Watkins made a note in his book. "Any other suggestions?"

"Not until we find out the identity of the body in the cave," Evan said.

"He might be Marshall."

Evan shook his head. "Too young," he said. "He only looked like a kid—university student type, wouldn't you say? I can't guess how he fits in."

"Different sort of crime, too," Sergeant Watkins said. "It's one thing to sneak up and push a bloke over a cliff. The person who did that obviously wanted it to look like an accident. Nobody would think a slit throat was accidental."

"A slit throat's usually desperation, in my experience," Evan said. "If you cut someone's throat, they can't make a noise. The murderer had to stop him in a hurry."

"From doing what, I wonder?" Sergeant Watkins looked up as a loud buzzing noise drowned out his words. "Great, this must be the lab boys," he said, getting to his feet as a helicopter came into sight. "HQ obviously thinks this is big stuff to be sending them in by helicopter."

P.C. Morgan came over to join them. "That's the last of the trippers gone down now, sarge."

"Good job, Morgan," Sergeant Watkins yelled over the noise of the landing helicopter. "You didn't see anyone who looked suspicious, did you? No bloodstain, no torn clothing?"

"Nothing, sarge. We watched them all very carefully. Of course the killer wouldn't have ridden down on the train, would he? There are a million places he could hide out up here, then make his own way down when nobody was looking."

"You're right, Morgan," Sergeant Watkins said. "I'll get onto the chief and ask if we can have the mountain searched, and we should keep an eye on the areas at the bottom of all the routes down too. He can't stay up here too long, not in this bloody weather."

"You want me to stick around up here?" Morgan asked.

"No, you can go on down, Morgan," Sergeant Wilkins said. "The lab boys will let us know when we can bring down the body. Tell Peters to go down with you and you two can take a look around in Llanberis. Ask at the station if anyone noticed a anything suspicious about the people getting off the train."

"And I should be getting down too, sarge," Evan said. "I get in trouble if I leave my station unmanned." He couldn't resist a grin. "You don't need me any more, do you?"

"I don't think there's much we can do, until forensic have gone over the crime scene," Sergeant Watkins said. "I'm heading down myself as soon as I can. I think it's time we checked on the whereabouts of this Mr. Marshall, don't you? I'll get onto the War Office right away and see what they can tell us about him."

"Right-o, sarge," Evan said.

"And I'll give you a call as soon as we know the identity of this latest body. Maybe he's our missing piece in the puzzle."

"I think we've got more than one missing piece right now," Evan said. "Even if we can link the men together, I've got no idea why anyone would want to kill them . . . unless the army can come up with some old feud." He paused then shook his head. "But even then . . . it takes a lot to make someone kill. And not only kill, but plan to kill. You have to be pretty desperate to do that."

"Or crazy," Sergeant Watkins said. "I just wish we hadn't picked up Daft Dai yesterday. It would have made it all so simple."

The helicopter disgorged its passengers. They ran clear of the whirling blades, carrying cameras, briefcases, and even a folded stretcher and made straight for Sergeant Watkins, their raincoats flapping in the strong wind.

"The chief says that Inspector Hughes is on his way back. We're not to move anything until he gets here," one of the men yelled to Watkins over the noise of the departing helicopter.

"Then he better bloody hurry up," Watkins snapped, looking up as he felt a raindrop on his face. "You'd better get all the lab work done as quickly as possible. By the time D.I. Hughes gets up here, the body will probably be washed out into the lake."

Evan started to move off, feeling superfluous. Most of the time he liked being a village policeman. Now it was being brought home to him that he had no business up here and that this crime was going to be solved without him. It made him wish for a moment that he hadn't resigned so impulsively from the investigation department before he had completed his training. If only he could have stuck it out, this might be him now, leading up an investigation. Of course, they had seemed like pretty compelling reasons to quit at the time . . .

He headed away from the group now following Sergeant Watkins cautiously down the steep path. The train had already made the trip down to Llanberis and had begun to climb again,

125

this time with more police on board. He wasn't going to wait to ride it down. It would be quicker if he took the Pig Track straight down to the village.

He was halfway down when it started to rain—not a fine misty rain, but big fat drops that soaked him in seconds. He regretted his decision to walk and was feeling a little sorry for himself as the large shadowy form of the Everest Inn came into view through the mist. As he dropped down to Llyn Llydaw he noticed someone was on the trail ahead of him, moving as fast as he was.

For a moment he thought it must be one of the policemen from HQ, coming down this way to make sure everyone was off the mountain. He increased his speed and saw that the person wasn't wearing a uniform. He was wearing cords and a tweedy jacket. Where the trails separated, above the village, the man kept on going and headed for the Everest Inn. It was then that Evan recognized him—Major Anderson.

Chapter 13

As Evan watched, the Major ran the last few yards to the inn and disappeared through a back door. With only a moment's hesitation, Evan ran after him.

Major Anderson looked up, startled, as Evan burst into his office. He had taken off his jacket and was now wearing a checked shirt.

"Oh hello, constable," he said. "Nasty weather, what?"

"Just up on the mountain, were you, major?"

"Yes, I was, as a matter of fact," Major Anderson said.

Evan glanced around the room to see if he could spot the major's jacket. He was still out of breath and couldn't come up with a good reason for asking to see it. Knowing the major, he wouldn't show it without a search warrant anyway.

"Do you mind telling me what took you up there this morning? And why you were in such a hurry to get down?"

The major gave him a withering look. "I should have thought that both were bloody obvious," he said. "I always go out for a morning walk if I can find the time. I like to keep fit, you know. It's good for the image of the place. I headed back down as soon as it started raining. I wasn't wearing rain gear and I was getting damned wet."

"Yes, I see your point," Evan said, feeling his own clammy clothes clinging to his cold body. "So you didn't get all the way up to the summit?"

"Nowhere near," the major said. "I don't have time for more than a brisk couple of miles—up one side of Llyn Llydaw (he pronounced it *Chlyn Chlydaw*, making it sound more like a couple of sneezes than Welsh words) and back down again."

"So you didn't get as far as Glaslyn and you didn't meet any policemen?"

"I say—what's all this about?" the major asked. "I thought I'd heard that you'd captured that insane chap. I've been telling my climbers that it was perfectly safe to go up there again."

"We captured the insane chap," Evan said, "and then we found another body this morning. So either Daft Dai has confessed to something he didn't do, or there are two murderers."

The major cleared his throat. "So, uh, was this man pushed over a cliff too?"

"No," Evan said. "I just wondered if you'd seen anybody acting suspiciously, major? Someone maybe with blood stains on his jacket?"

"No, good Lord, no," the major said emphatically. "I passed nobody. Of course you don't see much when the mist is down, do you? Another murder, you say? If this goes on, it's going to ruin us. Who's going to want to come here and risk being killed? You want to hurry up and catch him, constable!"

"We're doing our best, sir," Evan said. "And if we get co-operation from the public, it will go all the quicker, right?"

"Anything we can do to help, of course," the major said, opening his hand wide.

"You can tell your staff to keep their eyes open for anything suspicious." Evan focused his gaze on the major's hands. "Torn clothing, blood spots, anything that could be used as a weapon—"

"Good Lord, man. That would incriminate most of us here. Climbers are always tearing their clothing and scraping their skin. And they all carry pocket knives, I should imagine."

Evan nodded. "You've got a point there, major."

"Even I've got a couple of cuts on my hands," the major said, laughing easily. "Damned rope burn, actually. It's these new Dacron ropes. They're too thin for my taste."

"All the same, we'd appreciate it if you made a note of any possible clue you found. It's to your benefit as well as ours to get this solved quickly."

"Quite," the major agreed. "Now if you'll excuse me, constable, I really must go and change these wet clothes, and I think you should do the same, before we both catch pneumonia."

He put a firm hand on Evan's shoulder and ushered him out of the room.

As Evan walked back to the village, he considered the possibilities. The major certainly had the opportunity to kill all three men. He knew before anyone else that Tommy Hatcher was missing. He had been hurrying down the mountain today. But why? What possible motive could he have? Evan decided to call Sergeant Watkins and have him check the major's army record at the same time he checked the others. What if the major had been the officer held responsible for Danny's death? If his promising army career had been cut short, would that make him bitter enough to kill off the men he held responsible for letting Danny die?

Evan went straight to the police station and left a message on Sergeant Watkins' answering machine. Then he went home to change his sopping clothes.

"'Deed to goodness, what have you been doing to yourself then, Mr. Evans?" Mrs. Williams came rushing down the hall to greet him. There was no chance of sneaking into the house without her hearing the key in the lock. Evan thought she would have made a great police dog. She had a fantastic sixth sense that let her hear a footstep creeping past even when the TV was at full volume. "Look at you—soaked to the skin! Up the stairs with you and into a hot bath!"

"I'm fine, Mrs. Williams," Evan said. "I just need to change into dry clothes."

"A hot bath is what you need," Mrs. Williams said firmly. "You'll be catching your death of cold. Come on now, up the stairs with you."

Evan had no choice. Mrs. Williams marched up the stairs ahead of him and had already started running the bath for him. Alarmed that she might stay and supervise, he thanked her profusely, ushered her out, and locked the bathroom door. After he had peeled off his wet clothes, he was glad she had insisted. He lay back contentedly, feeling the life coming back into his frozen limbs.

He was still luxuriating in the tub when his pager beeped at him. Sergeant Watkins was a fast worker, he decided; Evan hadn't even expected him to be back at his desk yet.

He draped a towel around himself and ran to the phone.

"I didn't think you'd be back for hours yet, sarge," he said. "How did you manage to get back so quick? Fly?"

"How else," Sergeant Watkins said with a chuckle. "I

hitched a lift in the helicopter. No sense in getting soaked to the skin riding down in that blasted train. What's this about Major Anderson?"

Evan told him.

"Interesting," Sergeant Watkins said. "That's definitely worth looking into. He's only been here a little while, hasn't he? Maybe he took the job deliberately, so that it would give him a chance to . . ."

"To lure men here and bump them off?" Evan finished for him. "It sounds a bit far fetched to me, sergeant."

"I'd imagine the army makes a lot of blokes crack," Sergeant Watkins said. "Who knows—maybe he was stationed in Bosnia or in the Gulf War. He could have gone off his rocker. Anyway, I've put through the request for his records and we'll see what turns up, eh?"

"And when do you think we'll know more about the other young chap?" Evan asked.

"They should be bringing the body down within the hour," Sergeant Watkins said. "The helicopter went back with the police surgeon to bring him down. I'll give you a buzz— just off the record, of course. I've already had a phone call from Inspector Hughes telling me to wait for him before I do anything more. And knowing him, that means butt out and leave everything to him except bringing him cups of tea."

"One of that sort, eh?" Evan said sympathetically.

"And a great believer in physical evidence," Sergeant Watkins went on. "He reads too much Sherlock Holmes. He'll probably have us out scouring the mountain for toothpicks and cigarette packets. I just hope we get the information we want from the War Office before he gets here. Then at least you can do some private snooping while I'm stuck making his tea for him! I know you're dying to be in on this case!"

131

"I must admit I'd like to catch the man," Evan said. "I'll give you any help I can, sarge."

"Great. I'll call you back when I know anything more."

Evan put down the phone. The bath was now too cold to be enticing, so he dressed in dry clothes, noticing that Mrs. Williams had already whisked away the wet ones. She might be annoying, but there were definite advantages to having a landlady.

It wasn't until later that afternoon that Sergeant Watkins finally called back.

"Hello, sarge, I thought you might have been forbidden to talk to me," Evan said. "Did the D.I. get back then?"

"He's back all right," Sergeant Watkins said. "And barking orders at everyone like the bloody army. And speaking of armies—I've got the information you wanted. I've got a recent address for Marshall in Manchester, which is definitely close enough to have popped over here if he'd needed to. Oh and I thought you'd like to know—the army has no record of a Major Timothy Anderson."

"Is that a fact?" Evan couldn't resist smiling. "Goes around calling himself major, does he? But that shoots down my little theory about his being mixed up in Danny Bartholemew's death because he was the officer in charge. All the same," he went on, "it might be worth checking up on him, don't you think, sarge? A man who goes around calling himself something he's not might just be doing it for a reason."

"Possibly because he wants to give himself authority he doesn't otherwise have," Watkins said dryly. "It looks good on resumes, doesn't it? But it wouldn't do any harm to ask Scotland Yard to run a check on him."

"Have you got any details on that boy who was killed this morning?" Evan asked.

"Yes we have," Sergeant Watkins said. "Name's Simon Herries. Student at Oxford. Came up here alone for a climbing weekend. Liked getting away on his own, apparently—real sort of outdoor type. Family lives in Surrey. Dad's a solicitor. We spoke to the mother—very posh. Oh, and no family connection with the army."

"That's not much help at all, is it?" Evan said. "I don't see how we could link him in any way to the others. They were all very much working-class lads. What would an Oxford student have in common with any of them?"

"Maybe we were right about this just being a horrible coincidence," Sergeant Watkins said. "Maybe Dai really did push the other two over the cliff, or maybe somebody else bumped them off, and this was a different killer altogether."

"But why kill a nice young chap like him?" Evan asked.

"Search me," Sergeant Watkins said.

"Sarge, if your other murderer was hiding out on the mountain and this young bloke stumbled on his hiding place—he'd be desperate enough to kill wouldn't he?"

"Maybe," Sergeant Watkins said, "although you usually find that people who molest children don't go in for violence in the rest of their lives. I can't see him carrying around a knife like that, or slitting a throat. Stabbing in the back, yes, but slitting a throat—that takes guts and practice."

"So we're looking for someone who has killed before?"

"Or who was trained to kill?" Sergeant Watkins suggested.

"The army again," Evan exclaimed. "Anyone who had done commando training would know how to slit a throat."

"Pity about Major Anderson," Sergeant Watkins said.

"So where do we go from here?" Evan asked.

"I can't do much. The D.I. wants me standing to attention in case he needs me—needs a cup of tea, more like it. But you could do some checking on our Oxford student. We know he spent the night in the youth hostel in Llanberis. He's got it stamped in his hostel card. You could find out who he talked to and if he was seen with anybody this morning."

"Yes, I could do that," Evan said. "He'd have a photo on his hostel card, wouldn't he? Can you make me a copy of it? It's useful to jog people's memories."

"Yes, I can do that," Watkins said.

"I'll be right down then," Evan said, glancing at his watch. "And what about checking up on Marshall?"

"I've got the day off tomorrow," Sergeant Watkins said. "How about you?"

"You asking me on a date, sarge?"

Sargeant Watkins chuckled. "You're not my type! I thought I might take a drive in the direction of Manchester. I like to give my car a good outing at weekends. Care to come along for the ride?"

"Yes, I would," Evan replied. "Thanks, sarge."

"And Evans—just don't mention it to anyone else on the force, okay? D.I. Hughes has scheduled a meeting for this afternoon to go over his plan of action, as he calls it. I don't think he'd take kindly to us poking around on our own."

"You don't think you should put him in the picture as far as we've got and then get his blessing?" Evan asked.

"Good Lord no," Watkins said quickly. "Methodical Hughes? I told you, he's strictly by the book. He won't get around to admitting there might be a connection with the other murders for a week or two, and the other case is still his

134

number-one priority. I want to catch this chap while he's still around to be caught; it's all up to us, Evans."

"I'm game," Evan said. "See you tomorrow then. Who knows, maybe Marshall will confess, or give us the lead we want and we'll have the whole thing sewn up before your D.I. can start on it."

"Wouldn't that be nice?" Watkins chuckled. "Still, it's better than sitting around doing nothing."

When Evan hung up the phone, he opened the slim file he had assembled on the first two deaths. He took out the snapshot of Stew Potts and his wife. It wouldn't do any harm to show that around too. Maybe someone would recall having seen Stew going up the mountain railway or talking to someone down in the town. He was a good-looking chap, Evan thought. If he'd gone into any of the local shops or cafes, the girls working there would definitely remember him. Especially if, as his wife hinted, he had a way with the ladies.

He drove down to headquarters and collected a copy of Simon Herries' photo. He felt anger rising inside him again as he looked at the open, fresh face of the young man. Even in the small black-and-white snapshot he looked healthy and full of life. Who on earth could have wanted him dead?

Up in Llanberis, he showed the photo with very little success. The hostel warden remembered him, but said he had kept himself pretty much to himself. They'd had a noisy bunch in there last night—a party of German students who had got everybody singing. But this young chap had sat aside in an armchair, studying maps and making notes. One of the German girls had even teased him about it.

"You English are so quiet and shy," she had said.

135

Simon had smiled. "Not all of us, only me," he had answered and refused her invitation to join them.

The hostel warden couldn't remember Simon talking to anyone apart from that one line.

Evan had no more luck in town. Nobody recognized him in the stores or cafes. The girl in the supermarket thought he might have come in there to buy prepackaged sandwiches, but that was that. He was the sort of person nobody would notice, Evan thought. He'd probably have had quiet good manners and would want to slip in and out of places with the least amount of fuss.

Although Evan was sure it was a waste of time, he went to show the photo to the booking office clerk for the railway.

"When are they going to let us reopen?" the man demanded even before Evan could explain the purpose of his visit. He had a shrunken, sour-looking face and the thought flashed through Evan's mind that he could hardly be the best choice to greet tourists all day.

"They keep coming here, expecting to take the train and there's no trains running, are there?" he demanded. He had that belligerence of many small men. "We've got the place packed with tourists and they all want to go up the mountain and they're all angry with me because we're closed."

"Not until we've had a chance to search the entire crime scene," Evan said. "A man had his throat cut up there this morning. You wouldn't want someone else to end up the same way, would you?"

"The place is swarming with policemen," the booking office clerk said, frowning up at the mountain above him. "Nobody would be so bloody stupid as to wait around and be caught, would they? He's probably miles away by now."

136

"You didn't notice anything peculiar about anyone coming down on the train, did you?" Evan asked.

"They already asked me that a dozen times," the man snapped. "I told them that several thousand people pass through this station every day. I don't have time to go studying each of them."

"How about this lad?" Evan asked, producing the snapshot of Simon Herries. "Do you remember seeing him?"

The man shook his head. "No. Can't say that I do."

On an impulse Evan pulled out the photo of Stew Potts. "How about him?" he asked. "He was a big bloke. You might have noticed him."

The clerk stared at the picture. "Can't say that I remember him," he said. "I saw her, though."

Chapter 14

 Evan glanced up sharply at the railway clerk. "Her? You saw this woman?"

The man nodded. "Last weekend, I think it was."

"You're sure it was her?"

"Pretty sure. Foreign, wasn't she? Spoke with some kind of accent? Kind of tarty looking."

"That's right," Evan said.

The man was still staring at the picture as if he was trying to refresh his memory. "She came rushing up to me, just after the eleven o'clock train left the station. I told her she was unlucky. She'd have to wait two hours for the next one. Then she asked me if a big man with dark hair had taken the train."

"I told her what I told you. Hundreds of people pass me all the time. I don't have time to look at most of them. She hung around for a while, then she went away again."

"She wasn't with anybody that you could see?"

"No, she seemed to be on her own. But then someone

could have been waiting in a car for her, couldn't they? I didn't notice where she went or when she left."

"Thanks," Evan said. "You've been a lot of help. Sorry about the closed railway."

"I don't mind for myself," the man said. "I get paid the same wages if we run or not. But I don't like getting yelled at as if it's my fault. And I feel for Gwladys, too. She runs the snack bar up at the top and all her food's going stale on her."

"Where would I find Gwladys?" Evan asked. "She might have seen something too."

"She'd be home now, wouldn't she?" the man said. "Watching the telly. Addicted to telly, our Gwladys is. She lives for *Coronation Street*. You'd think those people were her relatives, the way she talks. We're always giving her a hard time about it."

He pointed out her cottage to Evan. Evan approached her front door hesitantly. The booking clerk had warned him that Gwladys would be more than annoyed about her food going to waste. But when she saw his uniform, her face lit up. "Come about the murder then, is it? You'd better come in then, hadn't you?"

She led him into a tiny, neat parlor. As had been predicted, the television was on in the corner.

"Sit you down," she said, pointing at a chair, piled with silky pillows. Evan sat, cautiously.

"I remember you," Gwladys said. "You were the one who bought two cups of tea this morning, weren't you?"

Evan didn't tell her how disgusting the tea had tasted.

"I wondered if you might be able to help us," he said. "You must see a lot from your little kiosk up there."

"Indeed I do," Gwladys said, nodding seriously. "You'd be amazed at what I see up there! You'd never expect those sort of things to go on up on a mountain, would you now?" She paused, her eyes widening. "You're not saying I might have seen the murdering brute with my own eyes, are you?" she asked. " 'Deed to goodness. To think I might have been up on the mountain alone with him. It makes the blood run cold, doesn't it?"

Evan produced both the photographs. Gwladys studied them both.

"This is the man, is it?" she asked, pointing at Stew Potts.

"Do you remember seeing him?" Evan asked.

Gwladys studied the photograph again. "Yes, I'm pretty sure I do. I remember thinking at the time that he looked like a shifty sort of character." She leaned closer to Evan and grabbed at his sleeve confidentially. "And the one he was talking to—I didn't like the look of him at all. That's a pair of bad 'uns, I remember telling myself. But you still could have knocked me down with a feather when I heard there had been a murder up there. Drug dealing maybe, but murder's something else, isn't it?"

"Could you describe the other chap he was talking to?" Evan asked hopefully.

"Like I said, a real criminal type of face he had." She focussed on Simon's picture. "And is this one of the gang too? He doesn't look the type, does he?"

"Do you remember seeing him? Early this morning, it would have been."

"Wait a minute. It's all coming back to me," Gwladys said, a big smile spreading across her face. "I think he was with the first man, and then they met the nasty-looking one."

"This morning?" Evan looked puzzled.

"I might be mistaken, of course," Gwladys said, "But I got a sort of premonition that a crime was going to be committed.

I went cold and clammy all over." She pointed to the pictures. "You want to find those two in a hurry and put them safely behind bars."

Evan concluded that the railway clerk had been right—Gwladys watched too much television. He'd come across this kind of thing before—someone who so desperately wanted to be helpful and involved that she'd say whatever she thought the police wanted to hear. Evan was fairly sure now that she hadn't seen any of the men or anything more suspicious than someone pouring away one of her cups of tea.

However he did have one good lead to go on now: The positive identification of Greta was quite genuine. When he got back to Llanfair he left a message on Watkins' machine, suggesting that they go to visit Greta in Liverpool on their way to Manchester.

It was almost six o'clock by the time Evan finally got back to the police station in Llanfair. Charlie Hopkins and Roberts-the-Pump waved as he passed them on their way into Red Dragon. A pint of Guinness was just what Evan needed right now. It had been a long, trying day. He was relieved to find no irate messages from Mrs. Powell-Davies and left a quick message on Sargeant Watkins' answering machine before heading over to the pub himself.

As he walked in the door of the public bar, he instantly regretted his decision. Being a Friday evening, the bar was full. As well as the local tradesmen, the farmers had congregated in one corner. Evan noticed a newborn lamb tucked in a shepherd's jacket and a sheepdog at his feet.

"There he is now, himself," Evan heard someone say and there was a sudden hush as all eyes turned to him.

"What's this we've been hearing then, Evan bach?" Charlie Hopkins asked. "They're saying there's been another body found on the mountain. So Dai shoved three of them over the edge then, did he?"

"Lucky we caught him before he could do any more harm, right Mr. Evans?" Cut-Price-Harry demanded, with a deliberate swagger for Betsy's benefit.

"It looks like we might have got the wrong man," Evan said as he joined them at the bar.

"But he confessed. That's what they were saying in the papers," Roberts-the-Pump said.

"He confessed all right, but he was in a cell last night and some poor boy was killed up there this morning."

"They're saying his throat was cut from ear to ear," Betsy looked horrified and delighted at the same time. "How terrible for you, Evan. I'd have fainted clean away if I'd seen something like that."

Evan was forced to admire the efficiency of the local bush telegraph. So far the police hadn't given out any details of the killing, but the people of Llanfair had found out anyway.

"A pint of Guinness for you, is it, Evan?" Betsy asked, already pouring the dark liquid into a tilted glass. "You don't expect to hear about violent killings here, do you?" she went on, putting the glass in front of him. "It's just like that film I saw last week about the Italian Mafia. Oh, it was horrible. I could hardly watch the things they did to one poor man to make him talk. Disgusting, that's what it was." She glanced up shyly at Evan. "It's still playing down in Caernarfon, if you want to go and see it with me—I wouldn't mind seeing it again."

"Thanks, but I've had enough of violence for the moment," Evan said.

143

"That's what I said when I came out of the cinema," Betsy said. "Next time I go to the pictures, I want a nice, quiet love story. Oh, and speaking of love stories . . . I already spoke to Mr. Harris and he says it's all right with him."

Evan stared at her, his mind racing. He had just noticed that she was wearing a silky white blouse with a black bra under it. What's more, the top three buttons were undone so that Evan had a glimpse of the bra peeking out. That was disconcerting enough in itself. But he couldn't think what she was talking about, and he wasn't entirely sure he wanted to find out.

"You are still going to do it, aren't you?" Betsy demanded. Evan was conscious of faces, watching him.

"Everyone's counting on you," Betsy added.

"Uh—what exactly are we talking about?" he was forced to ask. "I've had a very tiring day. My brain's not working too well."

"The dance, silly," Betsy said, laughing. "You and me—we're going to be chaperons, remember?"

"Oh, the dance. Right," Evan said. "I'm not sure if I'll be able to make it after all. Not now that we're in the middle of this new murder case. I promised the detective sergeant that I'd help him tomorrow. Who knows how late I'll be back . . ."

Betsy gave him a hard stare. "You just better be there, Evan Evans," she said. "Those children are counting on you, and I went out and bought a new dress. You're going to like it—it's very sexy." She smoothed her hands down over her waist as she said this, so that a good inch of black bra, and a lot of flesh, was visible.

"You hear that, Evan bach?" Charlie Hopkins exclaimed,

giving Evan a hearty slap on the back. "She's not going to let you wriggle out of this one. If you're still out with that detective, she'll come and find you and bring you back here!"

"I would too," Betsy said, over the loud laughter.

The next morning Evan left early to meet Sergeant Watkins in Caernarfon.

"Seen this morning's paper yet?" Watkins asked as they sped along the highway beside a gray ocean. He indicated the backseat of the car. Evan turned to retrieve the paper. ANOTHER BRUTAL MURDER HAS LOCALS TERRIFIED was the banner headline. Underneath in not much smaller type it proclaimed, "Local police understaffed and undertrained says local Member of Parliament. After four tragic deaths within the space of two weeks, local residents are afraid to go out of their houses." Evan's eye scanned down the column. The same local MP went on to suggest that Scotland Yard should have been called in immediately and hinted that the local police were not skilled enough to find the murderer.

"Your chief's not going to like this," Evan said with a grin.

"Too right he's not," Watkins agreed. "My word, are we going to be in for it on Monday. I'm just thankful it happened at a weekend. He'll have to wait until Monday morning to blow his top, unless he summons us all for a special meeting tomorrow."

"Did the D.I. turn up anything at Scotland Yard?"

"If he did, he hasn't told me," Watkins said. "And from the foul mood he's in, I rather think that he didn't. Between you and me, Evans, I'm rather thinking that maybe we've put all our eggs in one basket. We're assuming that this child molester, this Lou Walters, is the one we're looking for. We're following his mum and staking out his house. What if it wasn't him?"

"I suppose you have to go with the most likely suspect, don't you?"

"At least all the parents are keeping a close eye on their children right now, so he'll not find it easy to strike again around here," Watkins said. "I told the wife that Tiffany's not to go out alone ever, even if it's just across the road to her grandma's house."

Evan nodded. "You can't be too careful, can you?" he agreed. "The schoolteacher up in our village was telling her pupils the same thing."

As he said the words, a picture of Bronwen came into his mind and he remembered her cold gaze and the angry way she had parted from him. He had been so busy that he hadn't even had time to try and make things right with her. He wasn't even sure what he was supposed to say. It was always so complicated, dealing with women. That was one of the reasons why he had wanted to avoid any entanglements for a while, after moving from Swansea. His last experience was all too clear in his mind. He remembered the girl's expressionless face as she told him that she wasn't prepared to wait around until he was well again. It had hit him when he was at his lowest. He didn't want to go through anything like that again. Women, he thought, you're never really sure . . . which brought his mind back to the reason for their trip.

"I'll be interested to hear what Greta has to say for herself," he said.

"If it really was her," Watkins added. "You'd be surprised how many people are so anxious to help the police that they make up things."

"Oh, I wouldn't be surprised at all," Evan said, chuckling. "The old woman who served us that disgusting tea yesterday swore that she'd seen Stew Potts and Simon Herries together on the mountain yesterday, and they both looked as if they were up to no good."

"That's what makes our job so difficult," Watkins said, smiling too. "But what would Greta Potts have been doing around here? And why would she lie about it? If she was lying, she was a good actress, I'll give her that. She seemed completely surprised to hear that her husband had been in Wales."

"She'd have had as good a motive as anybody for bumping him off," Evan said. "She didn't trust him, she didn't like the way he ran around with other women, and she wanted to go home to Germany. One little push off a mountain would have solved all those things."

"And Tommy Hatcher? Do you think she pushed him too?"

"Maybe he saw her do it," Evan suggested. Then he smiled, shaking his head. "It is a little hard to take, I agree. But she came across as a determined woman, and a bitter one. And women are capable of anything when they're determined." He was thinking of Betsy, telling him that she was prepared to drag him to the dance, if necessary.

"That's for sure," Watkins agreed. "The missus has taken it into her head that we need a new washing machine. I keep telling her there's nothing wrong with the old one, but she won't give up on it. Every time we're out for a walk and we pass a shop, she has to stop and point out the washing machine she wants in the window. In the end I'm going to be so fed up with hearing about washing machines that I'm going to buy her one to keep her quiet."

"They usually manage to get their own way in the end, I notice," Evan said.

"You're not married yet, are you?"

"No. I had one close call. Now I'm taking my time," Evan said.

"Good idea. I'd had a drop too much one night and told Kathy that I could picture us spending the rest of our lives together, and she took it as a proposal. I suppose I must have meant it at the time, but next morning I was in a furniture store, picking out bedspreads and curtains. We had a deposit on a dining room set by the time we left the store and there was no way I could back out then. She's a nice woman, and our Tiffany's a lovely little kid, but I often wish I'd had more time to enjoy my freedom."

"I'm trying to hang onto mine," Evan said.

"You sound as if there's someone trying to make you change your mind."

"More then one of them," Evan said. "All nice girls, but . . ."

"Keep fighting, lad," Watkins said, chuckling. "This job is hard enough without the complications of coming home to a stopped-up toilet or a washing machine on the blink."

The mountains were receding behind them, as they crossed the flat coastal plain toward Chester and the industrial Northwest beyond. Evan could already see the brown line of pollution hanging across a pale blue sky. He couldn't imagine why anybody would want to live in a place like Manchester or Liverpool.

"Wouldn't it be great if Marshall turned out to be the one we were looking for?" Evan said.

"He's hardly going to confess to it, if he is," Watkins said. "And if he is, then we're dealing with a tough character. We've got to watch our step and tread very carefully. He mustn't think we're onto him. We're just curious to know if he got an invitation too and if he knows anything about this reunion and what it was for."

"Right, sarge," Evan said, nodding in agreement. "But we're going to do Greta first, aren't we?"

"Might as well. She's on the way and I'd like to hear what she has to say before we tackle Marshall."

Chapter 15

Greta Potts lived in a small, box-like semidetached house on a new housing estate about five miles from the center of Liverpool. The houses were all identical, with tiny squares of garden in front of them. Most of the gardens were a riot of spring flowers, and some had plastic gnomes on handkerchief-sized lawns. The English certainly love their gardens, Evan thought. The Welsh did too, but not as fanatically.

The small square of ground in front of Greta's house was paved over and boxed in with a chain between cement posts. He wondered whether Greta hadn't picked up the English fanaticism for flowers and lawns or Stew had been too occupied elsewhere. A car was parked outside the house and two little blond girls were sitting on the front step, playing house. They jumped up and ran inside calling, "Mama!" as they saw the two men approaching.

Greta was wearing jeans and an old T-shirt and came to the door with a mop in her hand. She wasn't wearing makeup today and her hair hung around her face. Evan thought she looked nicer this way, and younger too. He hadn't realized before that she was only in her midtwenties and he found he was thinking of her quite differently. It must be tough to find herself a young widow with two little kids in a foreign country, Evan thought.

"Yes?" She stared at them for a moment before she recognized them. "Oh, it's you," she said flatly.

"We have a few more questions we'd like to ask you about your husband's death," Sergeant Watkins said. "Some more evidence has come up during the week. Do you mind if we come in?"

Greta glanced back down the passage, as if making up her mind. "I suppose so," she said. "I haven't finished doing the living room yet."

The living room had a few toys scattered about on the floor, but it was otherwise spotless. Obviously Greta prided herself on her housekeeping because she rushed around, picking up the toys before inviting them to sit on a quilted satin sofa.

"I don't know why you came all this way," she said, perching on the arm of a matching satin chair. "I could have answered questions over the phone, and I already told you everything I know."

Watkins glanced at Evan. "We've come up with the name of another possible friend they went to meet," Evan said gently. "We just wondered if you'd heard of someone called Marshall."

"Jimmy Marshall? Oh yeah, I know him. He came to the house a couple of times. He lived not too far away—Manchester, wasn't it?"

Watkins nodded. "When was the last time you saw him?"

She wrinkled her nose. "I dunno. Ages ago—at least a year."

"And Stewart didn't get a phone call from him recently?"

"I wouldn't know, would I?" Her voice was sharp again. "He doesn't like me to use the phone when he's around. He says . . . he said that the phone was his business lifeline. He didn't want me tying it up chatting with my friends. So when he was home I always used to let him get it."

"And he didn't mention meeting Jimmy last weekend?"

"I told you," she snapped. "He didn't tell me anything about where he was going or who he was meeting. What's all this about anyway?"

Sergeant Watkins turned toward her. "Mrs. Potts, we're fairly sure now that your husband's death was no accident. That means that someone had to have a reason for wanting him dead."

Evan noticed she registered genuine surprise. "And you suspect Jimmy Marshall?"

"Let's put it this way, Mrs. Potts," Watkins went on. "There were four buddies that we know of, back in basic training days. Three of them are dead and, as far as we know, Jimmy Marshall is still alive."

She shook her head. "Not Jimmy. He wouldn't hurt a fly. Besides, why would he want to kill Stew? They were friends. They got along just great."

"That's what we're trying to find out, Mrs. Potts," Sergeant Watkins said. "Somebody wanted your husband and Tommy Hatcher dead. We need to know why. Can you think back and try to remember if there is anything at all he might have told you, any little incident from his army days, that might give us something to go on."

She shook her head. "Nothing. Nothing at all. The only time he talked about the army was about the base in Germany where we met. He had a good time there—it was real cushy duty and lots of good beer to drink. But he never spoke about what he did before. He was two years in Northern Ireland but he never spoke about that. He saw a car full of people get blown up and I know that stayed with him, because he used to have nightmares about it, but he'd never talk about it."

"Was Jimmy Marshall in Northern Ireland with him?" Watkins asked.

She shrugged. "I don't know where he knew Jimmy from. I got the feeling they were friends from way back." She got to her feet, clutching the mop she had rested against the chair. "Look, I'm sorry I can't help you more, but he's dead, isn't he? Talking isn't going to bring him back."

Evan got to his feet too. "You're right, Mrs. Potts, and I know this must be painful for you, but it would help if we could find your husband's killer, wouldn't it?"

"I still think the silly bugger slipped," Greta said. "I can't think of anyone who would have wanted him dead."

"He wasn't at all worried or apprehensive when he left on Sunday?" Evan asked.

"I didn't see him go," Greta said, going to peer out of the bay window to check on the little girls. "Where are those bloody kids? Oh, there they are. You can't be too careful these days, can you—not with so many lunatics around."

Evan opened the folder. "Here," he said. "This was the snapshot you gave us. I thought you might like to have it back."

"Oh, thanks," she said, taking it. "Sorry I couldn't help you, but like I said, he never told me nothing. Once he left this house, I never had a clue what he was doing."

"Is that why you decided to follow him that day?" Sergeant Watkins asked.

"What?" She stared at him as he she hadn't heard correctly.

"Your husband," Watkins said smoothly. "You followed him to Wales that day."

"Don't be so bloody daft," Greta said. "Why would I want to do that?"

"You tell us, Greta," Watkins said.

"You gave me the wrong photo, Greta love," Evan said. "You were on it too, remember? I showed it around and someone recognized you."

"Who?" she asked sharply.

"Ah, so you were there then?" Watkins demanded.

"I might have been," she said defiantly, "but I never talked to anybody."

"Except the man at the mountain railway station in Llanberis?"

He face flushed bright scarlet. "Oh, that rude bugger. Trust him."

"So you admit you were there, do you?"

She shrugged. "Doesn't seem any point in denying it now, does there? Okay, so I followed him. I just about had enough of him and his women. Some woman called him that Friday night. I overheard him talking to her and then he caught sight of me and went into some phony stuff about delivering orders. So I was sure that's where he was going on Sunday. I thought I'd finally catch him red-handed. I left the kids with a neighbor and I borrowed her car and followed him. You could have knocked me down with a feather when he drove to Wales. I watched him get on the mountain railway, and it looked like he was alone. I couldn't think of any woman who'd be silly enough to want to meet him on top of a bloody freezing mountain!"

"So what did you do after that, Greta?" Watkins asked.

"I hung around for a while to see if he came back down, but he didn't. So I drove home."

"You're sure about that—you came straight home? You didn't decide to follow him up the mountain on the next train?"

Her eyes became suddenly suspicious, darting around nervously. "Here, hold on a minute. You don't think I had anything to do with it, do yer?"

"You were one of the last people to see him alive, Greta. You've said yourself he was not the best of husbands," Watkins said.

"Oh, now look here." She was definitely flustered. "He drove me round the bend sometimes, but that doesn't mean I wanted him dead, does it? Use your head—why would I want Stew dead? Look at me now. I'm a widow with two little kids and no money coming in. I tried to talk him into taking out life insurance, but he wouldn't hear of it. He liked spending his money too much. So now what do I have to look forward to? We've got the payments due on the house and the car and the furniture. How am I going to make them—you tell me that."

"She does have a point," Evan said to Watkins as they drove away. "She's worse off without him than with him, even if he did fool around. What's she going to live on now?"

"Unless she's got a secret boyfriend she's not telling us about. She'll wait until the fuss has died down and then she'll quietly marry someone richer and nicer."

"How about if that was Jimmy Marshall?" Evan asked.

"She was definitely fond of him. You could hear it in her voice when she spoke about him."

"Wouldn't that be nice and tidy?" Watkins agreed. "She followed her husband to make sure he went up the mountain, called in Marshall, and he did the dirty work." He glanced at Evan. "You shouldn't have given her back that photo. We might need it as evidence."

"I made a copy first," Evan said, with a satisfied smile.

"Not as stupid as you look, are you?" Watkins said. "Now I'm going to be very curious to hear what Mr. Marshall has to say for himself."

Chapter 16

They found Jimmy Marshall in his back garden, mowing the lawn. A toddler scooted around him on a tiny bike making race car noises over the drone of the lawn mower. Jimmy stopped mowing as his wife led the two men out through French doors and yelled his name. Evan noted the pretty back garden with its blooming flower beds and manicured lawn. What he had seen of the house had been attractive too. Jimmy Marshall had definitely done better for himself than the others since leaving the army.

He came over to them—an amiable-looking man with sandy hair and freckles.

"Coppers, are you?" he asked, the smile fading as his wife introduced them. "Looking into Stew and Tommy's deaths?"

"You heard about them then?" Watkins asked.

Jimmy Marshall nodded. "Yeah. I couldn't believe it when I read it in the paper. What a shock! I suppose the silly buggers tried their hand at a spot of rock climbing when they were up there and pulled each other down, eh?"

"Does that sound like the kind of thing they would do?" Evan asked him.

Jimmy thought for a moment. "It sounds like the kind of thing Stew might have done. He was a right lad—always ready for a dare when we were in the army. You should have seen the scrapes we got into because of him. We were always on KP duty peeling bloody potatoes. But it was good for a laugh, I suppose. You needed to break the monotony somehow."

"You don't sound like you liked the army too much," Watkins said.

Jimmy Marshall shook his head. "I couldn't wait to get out. I only went in because my dad said I wouldn't be able to hack it. I'd have done anything to prove him wrong back in those days. But I hated it from day one. I'd never have survived if I hadn't made friends with . . ." His words drifted away and he shook his head. "I still can't believe it," he said.

"You knew about this weekend get-together then?" Watkins asked.

"Yeah, I was invited too," Jimmy Marshall said. "At least, I got this postcard with a picture of Mount Snowdon on it saying we were all going to meet for a memorial on the day Danny died."

"But you didn't go?"

Jimmy shook his head. "Nah. Too busy. I had to attend a conference in Chester all weekend for my firm. We got taken over by an American company last year and now we're into all this effectiveness and productivity training. We have to go to a couple of sessions a year. Retreats, they call them. Waste of time, I call them, but they're mandatory."

"And they can verify you were there all weekend?" Watkins asked.

"Oh yeah. They make sure you attend. We had to sign in

for each session," Jimmy said. "I was there all right, sitting on one of those hard chairs and suffering."

"Do you know who sent the invitation, Jimmy?" Watkins asked.

"I assumed it had to be Tommy Hatcher, because it had a London postmark."

"Did that seem the sort of thing you'd expect him to do?"

"I guess so," Jimmy said. "Tommy was the soft-hearted one. We used to tease him about it. But I never realized Danny's death had affected him so deeply. We never talked about it much, of course, but it was an accident after all, and accidents happen, especially in the army."

"Did you stay in touch with Hatcher or any of your other buddies after you left the army?" Sergeant Watkins asked.

"I saw Stew Potts a couple of times because he lived close by," Jimmy Marshall said. "In fact I've got a sympathy card on the table in there. I was in the middle of writing it to his wife, but I couldn't think what to say. What can you say?"

"And Tommy Hatcher?" Watkins asked. "Did you keep in touch with him?"

"No, I'd lost touch with him completely. That's why I was surprised he had my address."

"Any other mates from army days that you think might have been invited to the reunion?"

Jimmy Marshall thought for a moment, leaning on his lawn mower and staring out across the line of back gardens. Then he shook his head. "It was the four of us, really. I can't think who else would have been there . . . unless it was a bigger thing all together and they'd invited the whole intake, or even the whole hut."

"Who might have done that?"

"I've no idea. If it came from the army, it would have been

at an army establishment, wouldn't it? Besides, why would they want to hold a memorial for him? Half the top brass from the base got in trouble over it. They'd wouldn't want it raked up again."

"How about you," Evan asked. "Would you have gone if you could?"

Jimmy shook his head right away. "Nah. Not me. I don't go in for this sentimental stuff. I felt sorry for poor Danny, but what's the sense in dragging it all up again? It couldn't bring him back. It didn't make sense to me. It wasn't like he'd died a hero or anything."

"Tell me about that night on the mountain," Evan said. "The night Danny died. Anything you can remember."

"There's not much to tell," Jimmy said. "It was bloody horrible. We all had to get from point A to point B, across the mountain and down again. We'd only just started when a storm came in. It was blowing a gale, we were soaked through, and we could hardly see our hands in front of our faces."

"Wasn't it rather stupid to take people over the top of a mountain in weather like that?" Evan asked.

"We weren't supposed to go over the top. That was the funny thing," Jimmy Marshall said. "More like round the foothills. Danny must have got off course somehow, although he must have known that he was climbing higher and higher."

He glanced around. "Look, would you like to sit down? How about a beer, or a cup of tea?"

"Tea would be nice," Watkins said.

"I suppose you have to say no to the beer when you're on duty," Jimmy Marshall said with a grin. "Helen," he called. "Can you make us a pot of tea, love?"

"I made one, just in case," came the answering shout from the house, and Jimmy's wife appeared with a tray. There were

162

china tea cups on a lace cloth and a plate of assorted biscuits. "Here you are. You can pour for yourselves," she said, putting the tray on a small table.

Jimmy led them over and unfolded some plastic garden chairs. The toddler propelled himself over to them and immediately climbed onto Jimmy's knee. "Can I have a biscuit, daddy?" he asked.

"You'll spoil your lunch," Jimmy said, smoothing back the boy's unruly hair, "and mummy will be mad at me."

"Please?" the little boy draped his arms around the man's neck.

"Just one then," Jimmy said, giving him the only chocolate-covered one. The boy slid down and went running back to his bike.

"You've got a fine-looking little boy there," Evan commented.

Jimmy smiled, never taking his eyes off the boy. "He's a grand little chap," he said. "It's worth working your guts out for someone like him."

"They make you work hard then at your firm, do they?" Evan asked.

Jimmy nodded. "They want blood. It's like you're married to the bloody company. Helen gets right teed off about it. I'm away so much, you see."

"What kind of business are you in?"

"Computer marketing. I learned computer skills in the army and they've come in very useful, I must say. I got a job right out of the army, which is unusual up here. Twenty percent unemployment, we've got in these parts."

"It looks like you've done very well for yourself," Watkins commented.

"I can't complain," Jimmy Marshall said. He poured tea and handed each of them a cup.

"You were telling us about that night on the mountain," Evan said, taking the cup from him. "Were you supposed to be all together?"

"No. It was survival training. They sent us off at one-minute intervals. We were supposed to be using our compass and map-reading skills. Danny went ahead of me. I never saw him again. We didn't even know he was missing until the next day."

"Tell me about Danny," Evan said. "What was he like?"

"He was a nice kid," Jimmy Marshall said. "He was younger than the rest of us, but a real nice kid. He came from a rotten home, but he was determined to make something of himself. He used to tease us and say, 'When I get to be commander of this bloody camp, you're going to be sorry.' He was always joking that he'd be a general some day. I think he might have made it too. He certainly tried hard. The sergeants could never catch Danny slacking off. That's why I was surprised that it was him when they said a man was missing. I would have thought Danny had the smarts to get himself safely down again."

"So he got along well with everyone, did he?" Evan asked.

"It's funny you should say that," Jimmy Marshall said. "Normally he was always good for a laugh, but right before we went to Wales, he got all moody and he got into a fight with Stew one night."

"Over what?" Watkins asked.

"Stew made some joke about his family, I think. Usually Danny would have laughed it off, but he leaped on Stew like a wild thing. We had to drag them apart. It wasn't like him at all."

"And you say it was right before you went on the training exercises?"

Marshall nodded. "Funny, that. Almost as if he had a premonition of what was going to happen to him. He was that jumpy on the way there too. I remember the driver got really annoyed because Danny had to stop at God knows how many bathrooms. We were late in because of it." He paused, looking down at his tea cup. "Poor Danny. Now I think of it, maybe he wasn't well and he was hiding it. Maybe he should never have gone to Wales in the first place. Still, what good is it talking about that now? He's gone and nothing will bring him back."

Sergeant Watkins drained his tea cup and got to his feet. "Nice cup of tea, that," he said. "Thanks for all the information. You've been very helpful, Mr. Marshall. If you'd just give us the address of the place where you had this weekend seminar, we'd be grateful." He started to head back into the house. Evan followed him, his brain racing desperately to think if there was any other question they should have asked.

"Checking up on me, are you?" Jimmy Marshall looked half-amused. "I don't see what my being at a seminar has to do with a couple of blokes falling off a mountain." He stopped and Evan could almost see his mind making connections. "Hey, you suspect their deaths weren't accidents, don't you?"

"We're examining that possibility," Sergeant Watkins said.

"But who'd want to—" He broke off, then shook his head. "It doesn't make sense," he said. "They were both nice blokes."

"So you can't think of anybody who might want to give them a little shove off a cliff?" Evan asked. "No old enemies from army days?"

"Old enemies? The only enemy we had was that drill sergeant. What was his name? Stinks, that's what we used to call

165

him. Bad Ham Stinks! Apart from that we got along with everyone, I think. They used to like us because we were always in trouble. They used to say we broke the monotony."

They reached the front door and Jimmy opened it for them.

"What do you know about a man called Simon Herries?" Watkins asked suddenly.

"Simon?" Jimmy Marshall looked confused. "I don't know anyone called Simon. Posh kind of name, isn't it?"

"So you don't think he had anything to do with this reunion?"

"There was nobody at Caterick called Simon," Marshall said. "If there was, he'd have had the stuffing knocked out of him for having such a fairy kind of name."

"Thanks again, Mr. Marshall," Watkins said, extending his hand.

Jimmy Marshall shook it solemnly. "If someone did push Stew and Tommy off that mountain, I hope you hurry up and catch him," he said.

"We hope so too," Even said, shaking Jimmy's hand.

"He seemed like a nice enough chap, didn't he?" Evan commented as they drove away. "On the level, wouldn't you say?"

The detective nodded. "And he does have an alibi for the whole weekend too. Besides, what motive would he have? He clearly wants to put that part of his life behind him. He wasn't even going to go to the reunion."

"So we're almost back to square one again," Evan said. "Greta admitted she was there, but I can't see her having the strength to push two men off different cliffs, and she'd never have cut anyone's throat. Marshall was somewhere else all

166

weekend and doesn't appear to have a motive anyway. So who else is there?"

"I thought you were going to tell me, Sherlock," Watkins said, giving Evan a grin. "I tell you what—I'm dying for something to eat. You want to pull off and get a bite?"

"We just had tea," Evan reminded him.

"A couple of fancy biscuits. I didn't get breakfast this morning."

"Okay with me then, if you've got the time," Evan said.

Watkins grimaced. "The later the better as far as I'm concerned. I know I'm going to be whisked out to see washing machines the moment I step in the door. There's a good transport cafe just outside of Chester. All the truck drivers stop there. They serve coffee and tea in pint mugs. And that's just the small size."

Evan laughed. "Pull the other one, sarge," he said.

"You don't believe me? You wait," Watkins said.

About half an hour later he pulled off the road and drove into a huge parking lot full of trucks and cars. A neon sign was flashing above an undistinguished-looking building. May's Kitchen flashed in big red letters above Truckers Welcome in green.

"I hope you're hungry," Sergeant Watkins said as they got out. "They don't believe in small helpings."

They found a free table and Watkins ordered the breakfast special, even though it was already lunchtime. Evan followed suit. Almost immediately two pint mugs of milky coffee appeared.

"See, you didn't believe me, did you?" Watkins chuckled. "You wait until you see the size of the breakfast."

It also came up promptly, a big oval platter with three eggs, three long strips of bacon, three sausages, fried bread oozing bacon fat, a big pile of baked beans, fried tomatoes, and thick-cut chips, plus a tottering tower of toast to go with it.

"And I thought Mrs. Williams was overfeeding me," Evan commented as he attacked one corner of the food mountain. "There's enough cholesterol in this lot to kill every trucker in Northern England."

"Yeah, but it tastes good, doesn't it?" Watkins said, his mouth already half-full of sausage. "The wife is on a health food kick at home—grilled chicken, no skin, and lots of salad, so I stop here every time I get the chance."

The room shook suddenly. Even looked up. "That sounds like a pretty big truck outside."

"It's not a truck, it's the railway," Watkins said. "It goes under here in a tunnel."

Evan was feeling like a turkey stuffed for Christmas when they came out again. It had all been too greasy for him and he realized that he underestimated the quality of Mrs. Williams' cooking. She was, he realized, a very good cook. He must remember to tell her so.

As they got back into the car Evan noticed the road sign for Chester city. "You know, sarge," he said. "I've been thinking. Might it be an idea just to check up on Marshall's alibi? I'm sure he's on the level, but we're almost in Chester."

Watkins nodded. "It couldn't do any harm to check, could it? And that would definitely mean that the shops were shut by the time I got home."

They drove through an area of new factories until they stopped outside a glass and concrete building. The girl at the reception desk was very helpful. "We have to send the sign-in sheets back to the employer," she said, "but we always keep copies, in case the originals get lost in the mail."

168

She was gone a few minutes then returned. "What name did you want to look up?"

"Marshall. James Marshall," Watkins said.

The girl scanned down the page. "Yes, he was here Sunday morning, and Sunday afternoon," she said. "See, there's his name twice."

Watkins and Evan looked at the scribbled signature beside the girl's long red fingernail.

"Well, that answers that," Sergeant Watkins said.

"Here, hold on a minute, sarge," Evan said suddenly. "In the morning he signed himself J. Marshall and in the afternoon he signed James Marshall."

"What of it?"

"You usually sign your signature the same way, don't you? I don't think the same person signed this," Evan said. "Of course, I'm no handwriting expert, but look how he does his Js. Not quite the same, are they? And look at the line above—Jenny Prentice? Same J, isn't it? I think he got her to sign in for him."

Watkins was peering at the sheet now. "You know, you may be right," he said. "Which means that Marshall might not have been here on Sunday after twelve o'clock, and it's only an hour's drive to Llanberis."

"He's a damned good actor, I'll give him that," Evan said. "I'd have thought he was completely innocent."

"It's always the innocent-looking ones you have to suspect," Watkins said. "Let's give him a chance to relax and then we'll pay another call on Mr. Marshall and see how he's going to wriggle out of this one."

169

Chapter 17

"Here you are at last then," Mrs. Williams said, wiping her hands on her apron as she ran down the hallway to meet Evan. "Past four o'clock, is it just, and your dinner still waiting for you in the oven."

"Oh, Mrs. Williams, you didn't cook lunch for me, did you?" Evan said, feeling the meal he had just eaten still sitting like a lead weight on his stomach. "I told you I'd be out."

"And I thought you'd be wanting a good meal on your return. You must be famished, all the running around you do, and on your day off too! It's not fair the way they make you work," she said. She went ahead of him into the kitchen and opened the oven door. "I baked your favorite as a treat. Steak and kidney pie, is it? I know you like that."

Then, like a magician producing a rabbit from a hat, she reached into the oven and whipped out a huge steaming volcano of a pie with a golden brown crust. Rich brown gravy had oozed out of the vents she had cut in the crust and was trickling in thick, congealing rivers down the sides. She placed it on a trivet on the table and then reached in again to bring out a plate on which there were mounds of mashed potatoes, brussels sprouts, cabbage, and peas.

"Sit you down right away and get that lot inside your belt and you'll feel better," she said, "and while you're eating, I'll be ironing your best white shirt."

"My white shirt?" Evan's mind went blank.

"You'll be wanting to look your best tonight, won't you—for the dance?"

"Oh, the dance." With everything else going on in his life, the dance had once again completely slipped his mind. Now the full horror flooded back to him—all those little girls, trying to drag him onto the dance floor and then giggling at the way he danced, and Betsy, wearing a dress even she had described as sexy. Evan sighed. Life was very complicated.

At seven-thirty, feeling horribly self-conscious in a striped tie and a shirt that Mrs. Williams had starched to paper stiffness, Evan made his way through the village and up to the hall. The village hall was tucked in behind the school and Chapel Bethel. It was used for every function requiring space for more than twenty people, from Boy Scouts to the Women's Institute. It hadn't been built with atmosphere or festivity in mind. When Evan had first seen it, he had thought it had been built as a temporary structure, raised from the meadow below it on blocks. Its walls were merely asbestos panels nailed to a wood frame, its roof was corrugated iron, and it always felt cold and damp, although a two-bar electric fire was making a valiant effort in one corner. He was therefore surprised when he found it had been built before World War Two.

An attempt had been made to make it less gloomy for the dance, but it was like trying to dress up a pig as a French poo-

172

dle: There was no way to hide the innate ugliness. Mrs. Powell-Jones, Mrs. Parry Davies, and their crews had been busy with the crepe paper, winding it around the exposed cross beams, tacking streamers to the walls and wrapping the overhead lampshades in pink so that the light was muted and bathed the room in a pink glow. They had even made crepe paper flowers and tied bunches of balloons from the rafters. It was a gallant attempt but, Evan feared, a wasted one.

The village youth now stood huddled in two groups, boys at one end of the room, girls at the other. They were too busy looking at each other to notice the attempt at decoration. Between the two groups, along one wall ran a long table, covered in a white plastic cloth, adorned with more pink paper streamers. On this was a punchbowl containing pink liquid and plates of dainty sandwiches, sausage rolls, rock buns, frosted fairy cakes, and in the middle, slices of fruit cake. Evan suspected that the adults were way off the mark with their choice of food and that the young dancers would much rather have had tacos and pizza and crisps. But such foods had probably never even entered the Powell-Jones kitchen.

The music was coming from four big speakers, one in each corner, and it was very loud. Evan could feel the bass beat quivering through the floorboards and up through the soles of his shoes. He found himself wondering how there could be such a huge generation gap between himself and those who hadn't yet turned twenty. Evan had long ago decided that he had been born at the wrong time. He had never learned to like rock music. He loved the Beatles, even though they had already broken up by the time he knew what music was, but most stuff that came after them sounded like noise to him, especially the heavy metal that so many kids seemed to like now. One such number was playing as he walked in.

173

I'm goin' to kill ya. Uh huh. Uh huh.
I'm goin' to kill ya. Uh huh. Uh huh.

These seemed to be the only lyrics.

And they wonder why kids turn out badly, Evan mused. He crossed the room, carrying the plate of eccles cakes that was Mrs. Williams' contribution to the evening. Both groups looked up, making him feel like a Christian who had inadvertently strayed into a den of lions.

" 'Ello, Mr. Efans! Evening, Mr. Efans!" High voices echoed from the iron ceiling over the noise of the music.

Evan smiled and waved as he deposited the plate on the table.

"So good of Mrs. Williams," Mrs. Powell-Jones said, taking it from him and making sure it was put behind her own plate of fairy cakes. "Please make sure and thank her from me."

As if his entry was a cue, the two groups started to drift toward the middle of the room.

"Are you going to dance then, Mr. Evans?" one of the girls asked, while her friends giggled.

"I'm too old for your kind of music," Evan said. "I'm just here to keep you lot in order and make sure you behave yourselves all evening." He glanced swiftly around the group that now stood respectfully around him.

"Where's Dilys then?" he asked.

"I don't know," the cheeky girl said. "I was going to call for her at her house but she said she'd meet us here."

"She should be here by now," someone else said.

"Trust Dilys to be missing all the fun," another commented.

Evan didn't think that Dilys had missed too much so far.

"Well go on then," he said waving his arms expansively. "Don't just stand there. Start dancing."

"The boys haven't asked us yet," one of the girls said, glancing across at the tight knot of boys.

"Start dancing without them," Evan said. "You don't need partners for your sort of dancing, do you?"

The girls were giggling, but they did start moving around halfheartedly to the beat, their eyes on the boys all the time.

"They certainly do what you tell them," a voice behind him said. "You'd have made a good school teacher."

Evan turned to see Bronwen standing there. She was wearing a long denim skirt and a blue-and-white smocked peasant tunic over it. She looked ridiculously young and he realized she must have been here all the time, among the girls, without his noticing her.

"Bronwen!" he stammered, completely caught off guard. "What are you doing here?"

"They're my former pupils," she said, laughing at his embarrassment. "Why shouldn't I be here? I know them better than anybody. Don't you think I should supervise their dances?"

Evan couldn't think of anything to say to that. He was chiding himself that it had never crossed his mind that Bronwen would be at the dance. With a sinking heart he realized that any minute now the door would open and Betsy would walk in . . . and expect him to dance with her. What would he do? Betsy wasn't the kind to take no for an answer. She'd be quite prepared to drag him, protesting, onto the dance floor.

He had only just finished thinking this when the door opened and Betsy entered with a great swirl of wind that sent the streamers flapping and napkins flying off the table. She was wearing a fake leopard coat, which she held closed up to her chin. She stood framed in the doorway for a moment, then she made her way across the middle of the room, walking carefully over the uneven floorboards in four-inch spiked heels. She walked right up to Evan, then let the coat slide off bare shoulders. The dress was black spandex, very short with tiny straps. To say it fitted her like a glove would be an understatement. It left nothing to the imagination.

"Hello, Evan," she said. "I managed to get away like I said I would. How do you like my dress then?"

"It's . . . uh . . . very striking." Evan managed to keep his voice steady. He now saw why no heating system was needed in the hall. He could feel the sweat trickling down his back.

"Oh, is that your dress?" Bronwen asked. "I thought it was your underslip."

Betsy's gaze moved to Bronwen, like a searchlight cutting through the darkness. "What's she doing here?" she asked Evan.

"I was about to ask the same thing," Bronwen said. "I didn't realize you were still a teenager, Betsy. You must have left school awfully early, but then I suppose you never put much importance on book learning, did you?"

"I'm here as official chaperon, Bronwen Price," Betsy said. "Constable Evans asked me to come and give him a hand, and I can never refuse Constable Evans, can I, Evan bach?"

"I hardly think that dress is suitable for a chaperon," Bronwen said.

"It's a dance dress, isn't it? And this is a dance."

"You're supposed to be supervising them, not leading them astray," Bronwen said.

"I've nothing to be ashamed of in my body, Bronwen

Price," Betsy said. "Even young boys like a woman to look like a woman, don't they? Not like a shapeless sack of potatoes." She slipped her arm through Evan's. "How about you and me get the dancing started, eh, Evan bach? We'll show them how the grown-ups do it!"

Evan was trying to make his brain work and to keep his eyes off Betsy's dress.

"I'm sorry, Betsy love," he said in a flash of inspiration, "But I already promised Mrs. Powell-Jones that I'd be in charge of the punch. In fact I see her beckoning me right now, so I'd better get over there before she starts yelling, hadn't I?"

He realized he was probably being a coward as he slipped between Bronwen and Betsy and made his way to the punch table, leaving the two girls glaring at each other like two boxers who have just climbed into the same ring.

"I'll take over from you here, Mrs. Powell-Jones," he said, almost snatching the ladle from her grasp.

"Oh no, that's quite all right, Mr. Evans," Mrs. Powell-Jones said. "I'd better do it myself. It's so hard to clean up sticky floors in here."

"I've got a very steady hand—ask anyone who drinks with me at the Red Dragon," Evan said, "and you know the young people much better than me. You should be out there, mingling with them, getting them to dance."

"Well, it's true they have mostly come through my Sunday school classes," Mrs. Powell-Jones said, looking around hesitantly.

"Mrs. Parry Davies certainly seems to be getting along famously with that group in the corner," Evan said.

"You're right. I should be mingling more," Mrs. Powell-Jones said. "I'm just so used to giving myself the humble task. I was born to be Martha and serve. But if you're really offering, constable, then I should make the young people welcome as they come in."

She handed Evan the ladle. "And I'd offer my congratulations on catching that lunatic so speedily," she added. "It is certainly a relief to sleep knowing that my house and my garden and my apple pies are inviolate once more."

Evan watched her cross the room and saw the anguished look on the faces of the boys she went to join. He felt sorry for them, but it was better than their having to watch himself in a three-way battle with Bronwen and Betsy. He found himself thinking about Daft Dai. He supposed it was very possible that he had been the one responsible for peeping in Mrs. Powell-Jones' window and stealing her apple pie, even if he'd had nothing to do with the murders. At least that's one small crime solved, he thought, even if we're a long way from solving the other ones.

At ten o'clock, the dance was in full swing. Either the boys had lost their shyness or they had decided that dancing with the girls was a lesser evil than being polite to Mrs. Powell-Jones, but the floor was now full of twitching bodies. Every face was very red, as Mrs. Powell-Jones allowed no slow numbers, in case the boys and girls got too close to each other. Evan had done a huge trade in punch and was on his third bowl. Betsy kept slipping behind the table next to Evan with the excuse of offering to hand around plates of sandwiches.

"Nobody seems to be eating the cheese and pickle," she'd say. "I better take them around before they go stale." She peered into the punch bowl. "It's getting low again, isn't it?" she asked. "Do you want me to mix up some more for you, Evan bach?"

"It's okay. I can do it," Evan said.

"I think it's criminal, the way that Powell-Jones woman has kept you working all evening. It's your day off, after all. She should let you have at least one dance."

"It's okay, Betsy. I don't mind. And standing here lets me keep a good eye on the kids too."

"I tell you what, Evan Evans," Betsy said. "Before this evening is over, I'm going to that stereo player and I'm putting on a slow number and you and I are going to dance. No excuses!"

Then she swept away with a tray of sandwiches. Evan sighed. Bronwen would never understand, he was sure. And yet if he danced with Bronwen and snubbed Betsy, the whole village would have him engaged to her by the end of the evening and he wasn't sure he wanted that either. He'd have to come up with a gracious way out somehow.

Evan's gaze swept over the dancing teenagers. Dilys hadn't shown up after all, he noticed. Her fear of being teased had won out over her desire to dance with him. Poor Dilys, he thought. He could remember what it was to feel different and to know that people were laughing at you. He remembered those first terms at Swansea Grammar School very well. They had made fun of his accent, his lack of English, his skinny legs, his haircut, just about everything. He could definitely understand why Dilys had stayed away tonight.

At that moment the door opened and a group of mothers came in. They stood in the doorway with tolerant, proud smiles on their faces, watching their children dancing. There was a pause in the music and the youngsters made a rapid dive for the food table, pretending not to notice that their mothers had now arrived. Then one of the mothers came scurrying across the room after them.

"Where's Dilys?" she demanded.

Blank faces turned to her. "Dilys? She hasn't been here all evening, Mrs. Thomas," one of the girls said.

"But she left the house at seven o'clock," Mrs. Thomas said, the panic rising in her face. "I heard the front door go. You mean she never got here? Nobody's seen her? What can have happened to her? Where can she be?"

Chapter 18

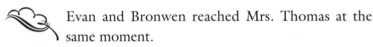 Evan and Bronwen reached Mrs. Thomas at the same moment.

"Don't worry, Mrs. Thomas," Bronwen said in a calm voice. "I'm sure there's a perfectly reasonable explanation. You know what silly things children get into their heads sometimes."

"That's right, Mrs. Thomas," Evan agreed, sounding more upbeat than he felt. "She was telling me the boys teased her about her height. I bet she got cold feet at the last moment and she's hiding out until the dance is over."

"But I heard her go out," Mrs. Thomas insisted. "Where could she have gone?"

Evan looked around the scared faces. "She didn't say anything to any of you?" he asked. "She didn't have any secret plans we ought to know about?" There was silence. A few girls shook their heads.

"Come on, girls," Bronwen said. "You're not helping Dilys

by keeping anything from us right now. We need to find her. Glynis, you're her friend, aren't you?"

"But Miss, we all thought she was coming here," Glynis exclaimed. "She was supposed to call for me at my house and we were going together. Then she phoned this evening and said she'd come on her own and I was to go on without her."

"Did she say why?" Evan asked.

Glynis shook her head. "I just thought she was taking a long time getting ready maybe. She's an awful slowpoke sometimes."

"So she was definitely planning to come here then?" Evan went on.

The girls looked at each other, then nodded agreement. "She was looking forward to it, Mr. Evans," one of them said. "She said you'd told her that you'd dance with her." She blushed furiously. "We were all a little jealous, you know."

"We talked about what we were going to wear on the bus yesterday," another girl said. "And Dilys said she'd bought a new silky blouse specially for the dance."

Mrs. Thomas clutched at Evan's sleeve. "What are we going to do, Mr. Evans? Something terrible's happened, I know it."

"Don't worry, Mrs. Thomas. We'll get everybody out looking for her right away," Evan said, trying to stay calm himself.

"But where could she have gone?" Mrs. Thomas wailed. "Why isn't she here?"

Evan looked around the room. "Betsy love, run down to the pub and tell all the men we need them this minute. We've got a missing little girl we have to find," he said.

Betsy didn't wait to argue. She grabbed her coat and fled out of the door.

"I really think that I should maybe question these children," Mrs. Powell-Jones said, pushing through to stand beside Evan. "I am very good at knowing when a child is lying."

"Thanks a lot, but Constable Evans is already handling this just fine," Bronwen said firmly. "Why don't you make Mrs. Thomas a cup of tea?"

Mrs. Powell-Jones opened her mouth to speak again, then shut it and stalked in the direction of the kitchen. It seemed only a few seconds later that there was the sound of boots on the steps and the men appeared. Mr. Thomas, his face ashen, pushed through to his wife.

Evan divided everyone present into search parties and they spread throughout the village. Evan stood on the hall steps, hearing high voices calling out, "Dilys, where are you?" and Mrs. Thomas' plaintive, "Dilys love, please come out if you're hiding," as they moved off down through the village.

In the darkness Evan could make out the yellow police tape across the paths that led to the mountain. He didn't want to think the unthinkable, but he couldn't help it. Dilys' hopeful face flashed into his mind and he heard her clear young voice saying, "I was hoping you'd dance with me once."

He borrowed Mrs. Powell-Jones' flashlight and took it upon himself to check around the hall and the area beyond that led to the mountain trails, but he found no obvious clues in the dark. One by one the search parties returned having found nothing. The teenagers were looking white-faced and tired.

"You might as well all go home," Evan said. "There's nothing more we can do tonight. I'll go down to the station and get onto headquarters. They'll notify all units to be on the lookout for her." He turned to the Thomases. "And if you don't mind coming down to the station with me," he said. "I'll need your help to fill out a report and get all the details on her."

"We've got young Melanie home alone," Mrs. Thomas said, her voice rising in fear again. "I don't like leaving her."

I'll go and stay with Melanie until you're done," Bronwen said. She shepherded Mrs. Thomas down the hall steps and started down the street with them.

"You're very kind, I'm sure, Miss Price," Mrs. Thomas said, attempting a grateful smile.

Bronwen touched her arm. "Try not to worry too much," she said. "I've known girls do very silly things before now. It might turn out to be something no worse than sneaking down to Caernarfon to see a forbidden movie."

"But Dilys has never done a thing like that," Mrs. Thomas said. "She's always been such a good girl."

A lone streetlamp threw an anemic glow down the village street. It was the sole source of illumiation until the light that streamed from the pub windows, farther down the hill. Evan had complained about the poor street lighting before. Anyone could sneak anywhere without being seen. He could feel dread rising in his throat.

"Has she been acting strangely at all recently?" Bronwen asked gently as they reached the Thomas' cottage. "Has she been at all sneaky or secretive? Has she got any new friends from outside the village?"

"Not really," Mrs. Thomas said. "Not that we know of, anyway. She's been moody lately, but that's just a stage they go through when they're teenagers, isn't it?"

"So you can't think of anything that might have happened to make her change her mind about the dance?" Evan asked.

"No, she was looking forward to it," Mrs. Thomas said. "She talked about nothing else all week."

"So tell me about this evening," Evan said. "How was she

acting earlier? Did you all have dinner together? Was she still excited about the dance?"

"Well no, we had a little upset right before suppertime," Mrs. Thomas admitted. "Dilys and her sister had one of their little spats and her father had to show them both who was boss."

"She ran off to her room crying and wouldn't come out again," Mrs. Thomas went on. "But that wasn't anything unusual. They're always getting into fights and Dilys is always making dramatic exits to her room."

"That sounds like a typical teenager," Bronwen agreed. "So you didn't actually see her before she went to the dance?"

"No, she stayed in her room and she wouldn't come out for supper," Mrs. Thomas said. "I didn't worry too much. I knew there was plenty of food at the dance. Then Mr. Thomas and I were in the living room watching TV and we heard the front door slam and we assumed it was Dilys going to the dance." She grabbed her husband's arm. "Why did we let her go without saying good-bye to her? I'd give anything . . ."

"Don't upset yourself, mother," Mr. Thomas muttered. "She'll show up."

"I'm sure she will," Bronwen said. "I'll go on in and sit with Melanie."

"She should be asleep," Mrs. Thomas said, glancing at her house, "although I wouldn't put it past the little monkey to sneak down and watch the telly again the moment we were out of the way. She's going to be the wild one, Miss Price, as I expect you know."

"Let's get on down to the station, shall we?" Evan suggested.

It was cold in the little room and Evan turned on all three

bars of the electric fire. Even so he noticed that Mrs. Thomas couldn't stop shivering. "This won't take a minute," he said, "Then you can make yourself a nice cup of tea when you get home."

"You're very kind, Mr. Evans," Mrs. Thomas said. Evans always marvelled that people didn't lose their good manners even in moments of great stress.

The Thomases sat like two statues. Only Mrs. Thomas gave him the answers to his questions, but she always looked to Mr. Thomas for his confirming nod. After the form was completed Evan called the information through to headquarters. He was glad that they couldn't hear the dispatcher on the other end of the line. "A young girl missing again?" he asked. "That doesn't sound good, does it?"

Evan had trouble sleeping that night. When he did doze off, his dreams were so disturbing that he shook himself awake again. He was glad for an excuse to get up when his pager beeped at six.

"What's this about a missing girl?" Sergeant Watkins' voice came on the line. "I just got called in on my day off."

Evan gave him the details.

"Christ," Watkins muttered, "and we've had a definite sighting of Lou Walters too. He was trying to get to his mother's house and then they lost him again. He seems to know the mountains well."

Evan's heart sank. "Is there anything I can do, sarge? She's the nicest little girl . . ."

"There's nothing you can do that we're not already doing," Watkins said. "The chief's sent out every available unit. If she hasn't told any of her friends that she was going somewhere, you can bet your life she wasn't intending on going."

186

"They all seemed as surprised as we were," Evan said. "I don't think anyone was doing any covering for her."

"What about friends outside the village?" Watkins asked. "Is there anyone she might have decided to go visit—anyone from school? Any relatives?"

"No one from school, as far as we know. She has an auntie in Liverpool that she's fond of, but we've already contacted her."

"Doesn't sound good," Watkins said, echoing the dispatcher's words. "I'll let you know if we hear anything. Lucky the chief kept the mountain sealed off, isn't it? It would be hard for anyone to get up there without one of our men spotting him."

After he had dressed, Evan hurried downstairs and intercepted Mrs. Williams before she could cook him a big breakfast. He found it hard even to swallow a cup of tea.

I should be doing something, he kept on telling himself, but he had no idea what. Every squad car of the North Wales police was already out looking for her. He felt useless and angry.

At nine o'clock he called back Sergeant Watkins. "Listen, sarge, any objection to my going back to see Jimmy Marshall? We need to hear what he's got to say about the forged signature, don't we? And I'd rather all of you detectives kept looking for Dilys."

"Fine with me. Go ahead," Watkins said. "It might be a good idea to catch him off guard before he hears that we were checking up on him and has had time to think up a story."

"Right. I'll drive over there straight away," Evan said.

"Oh, and Evans," Watkins added. "Go carefully, won't you? If it did turn out that we've found our murderer, he's already killed three men."

"Don't worry, sarge. I won't let him take me up any local mountains to show me the view."

Watkins chuckled as he hung up. Evan went to his car, glad to have a task that he could do. He drove fast, keeping at the motorway speed limit and ignoring the complaining whine of his aged engine.

Jimmy Marshall was watching cricket on the television. He looked up in surprise as his wife ushered Evan into the living room.

"Back again so soon?" he asked.

"Sorry to disturb your Sunday," Evan said, "but there was one little point I wanted to clear up with you."

"If you'd forgotten to ask me something, you could have called me, you know. They have phones in North Wales, don't they?" Jimmy grinned good-naturedly. Evan noticed that he seemed relaxed enough. "Can I offer you a beer today, or are you still on duty?"

"I won't have anything, thanks," Evan said. "Who's winning?" He indicated the screen.

"Yorkshire, beating Surrey," he said. "I always like to see Northerners show the South a thing or two." He looked away from the set. "What was it that was so urgent you drove all the way over here on a Sunday? You didn't find my fingerprints on a mountaintop, did you?"

He was still smiling. "Nothing like that," Evan said. "I just wanted to know if you had a good excuse for skipping class last Sunday afternoon—you know, when you had someone forge your signature in the book at that seminar place?"

For a second Jimmy's face went pale. Then he nodded. "You're sharp, you chaps from Wales, I'll give you that," he said. "As it happens I do have a good excuse—and nothing to do with going up mountains, either."

"I'm listening," Evan said.

Jimmy looked around. "Don't let the wife hear," he said, lowering his voice.

"You went to meet a woman?" Evan asked.

Jimmy chuckled. "Nothing like that. It's harmless really, but it could get me into trouble at work. Look, I told you that we've been taken over by this American company, right? They're into all this self-motivation nonsense. I don't go in for all this touchy-feely, sharing-your-innermost-feelings stuff. I couldn't take any more of it by Sunday afternoon. I mean, would you want to sit in a circle and hug the person next to you and tell them that you liked them just the way they are?" He made a pained face. Even had to smile.

"So you cut class?" he asked.

"I had someone sign in for me. I didn't think they'd ever check," Jimmy said.

"And where did you go?"

Jimmy looked sheepish. "I went to the pictures," he said. "Arnold Schwarzenegger was playing in Chester. My wife hates action movies. If we go at all, it's always Jane Austen and that kind of thing. So I took my chance."

"Can anyone back this up?" Evan asked.

"I doubt it. I mean, you don't notice people going into a cinema, do you? But I'll repeat what I said yesterday. Those men were my friends. What possible reason could I have for wanting either of them dead?"

Evan nodded. "I suppose I'll have to take your word for it then," he said. He got up. "Sorry to have disturbed your Sunday, but we have to follow up every lead we get."

"I understand," Jimmy Marshall said. "They don't give you much time off, do they?"

"I don't mind," Evan said. "If there's a dangerous man

189

running around, I'd rather see him safely behind bars than get my days off. And speaking of dangerous men . . . were you at work last Friday?"

"You mean the Friday just gone by?" Jimmy Marshall looked puzzled. "I was down in London, doing a presentation to clients. I went down on Thursday and came back Friday afternoon. What did you want to know for?"

"Just a little thought," Evan said. "And you can prove you were down in London, I suppose. You didn't get anyone to forge your signature down there?"

Jimmy Marshall laughed. "No chance," he said. "I was teamed up with a character called Billy Patterson and he's the most obnoxious little prick you could ever meet. Talk about a stickler for rules and procedures! And a right crawler too—he'd report me to head office if I overcharged by ten pence on my expenses. We even had to share a room at the hotel and he snores. I can give you the name of the hotel and the address of the clients we met if you want to check on me."

"Thanks. I'd appreciate that information," Evan said. "We have to follow up on everything, you know."

"I understand. If my friends were murdered, I'd like to see the killer caught as much as you would." He went over to a desk in the corner and scribbled down phone numbers on a sheet of paper. "It'll all check out," he said, handing it to Evan. "Good luck. I hope you catch him." He shook Evan's hand.

Evan drove back feeling satisfied that at least one part of the investigation had ended the way he wanted it. He had liked Jimmy Marshall from the beginning. He hadn't wanted to think of him as a possible murderer. And he understood Jimmy's motive for deception completely. Only once in his life he'd had to attend one of these psychological seminars. It had been back in Swansea when they had brought in outside behaviorists to make the police image more positive with the public. Evan had found the session excruciatingly painful. It might be fine for Americans to go up to strangers and say, "Hi, I'm Evan. I want to be your friend," but the British were raised to be reserved. They could travel on the same commuter train for thirty years and only raise their hats to each other. They would never presume to start a conversation.

He had been deep in thought when his engine developed a higher-pitched whine, reminding him that he should check the oil. The old clunker had been burning a lot lately. He pulled into the slow lane and dropped his speed to fifty until he got to the next exit. He was negotiating the off-ramp when he glanced across the road. Someone was standing at the on-ramp on the other side, thumb hopefully out and waiting for a lift. He drove by too quickly to be sure, but Evan could have sworn he'd just seen Dilys. Evan braked and turned to look back, getting an angry honk from the driver behind him.

He waited impatiently for the traffic light at the underpass to turn green, praying that nobody had picked her up before he got to her. He shot forward as the light changed and came out of the underpass to see a VW van pulling up beside the girl. He screeched to a halt behind the van and jumped out.

"Dilys!" he yelled.

Dilys looked up with big, fearful eyes.

"Where do you think you're going?" he demanded. "We've got half of Wales out looking for you."

"I'm going to my auntie's house in Liverpool," she said defiantly. "They don't want me at home any more. I've run away."

"Don't be so silly," Evan said, realizing as he said it that this probably wasn't the most tactful way to talk to her.

"You don't have to go with him if you don't want to," the

191

driver of the VW van called to her, opening the van door. "You've got rights, you know."

Evan stalked over to the young van driver, badge in hand. "Go on, get moving," he said angrily," or I'll book you for parking illegally."

The van moved off, leaving Dilys clutching her bag protectively to her chest. "Come on, love," Evan said quietly. "Get in the car and we'll go and get a cup of tea. I don't suppose you've had much to eat today, have you?"

"Only a Crunchie Bar," she said. She let him take her knapsack and lead her back to his car. "But I'm not going home," she said defiantly. "I've had enough of being treated badly."

Evan got in beside her and they drove off slowly. He didn't say any more until they were seated in the same transport cafe where he had eaten with Sergeant Watkins and Dilys had a big mug of tea and a hamburger in front of her.

"They treat you badly at home then, do they Dilys?" Evan asked quietly.

She nodded. "It's not fair," she said and her voice caught in a sob. "They never take my side. It's always her. Melanie can't do anything wrong, can she?"

"Your sister?" Evan asked.

Dilys nodded again. "They like her better than me. They wouldn't even care if I wasn't around any more," she said.

"Did something happen that made you decide to run away all of a sudden?" Evan asked. "Or have you been thinking of this for a while?"

She stared down at her plate, idly dipping a chip into a large puddle of tomato ketchup. After a while she said, "I caught her reading my diary, Mr. Evans. My private diary that I keep in my undies drawer. It's got a lock on it and everything, and she was reading it. Wouldn't you get angry if that happened to you?"

"Definitely," Evan agreed.

"I was so mad that I just lost my temper," Dilys went on. "I snatched it away from her and I started hitting her. She screamed and Mum came running and dragged me away from her. There was an awful row. My dad told me I was a big bully and he'd give me a good thrashing if I ever touched my sister again. He said he'd a good mind to make me stay home from the dance as a punishment."

"But he didn't hit you?" Evan asked.

Dilys shook her head. "He always threatens to hit us, but he never does."

"That sounds pretty normal to me, Dilys," Evan said. "Most parents yell at their kids if they've been fighting, don't they?"

"I don't mind the yelling," Dilys said. "It's just that it's always so unfair. They never listen to my side, Mr. Evans. She's always bugging me and telling tales on me and it's always me who's wrong." She looked up to meet his gaze. "I know I shouldn't have hit her, but she deserved it. She had no right to go snooping into my diary, Mr. Evans. She poked her nose where it had no business to be and she got what was coming to her, didn't she?" She picked up her hamburger again and took a big bite. "I don't want to go back there, Mr. Evans. I want to go to my auntie. She likes me."

"Your parents like you too, Dilys," Evan said. "Your mother was going half crazy last night, worrying that something had happened to you. We had the whole village out searching for you and now half the North Wales police force is driving around looking for you."

"Seriously?" Dilys looked rather pleased.

Evan fished into his pocket and brought out a handful of change. "There's a phone on the wall. Why don't you go and give your mother a call and let her know that you're all right?"

Dilys got to her feet. "Okay, Mr. Evans," she said with a little smile.

Chapter 19

Evan arrived back in Llanfair to find himself welcomed as a hero once again. As he watched Dilys run to her mother's arms and even the silent Mr. Thomas reach out to ruffle her hair, he decided that it was moments like this that made him glad he was a policeman. If only the real crimes were as easy to put right, he thought. If only every scare ended as happily . . .

There was almost a party atmosphere in the village as the news of Dilys' safe return got around, but Evan was not feeling in a party mood. He glanced up at the sky. White puffball clouds were racing past the mountain peaks and a fresh spring breeze was blowing. Snowdon was definitely beckoning, but unfortunately, it was still off-limits. D.I. Hughes was known for being exceedingly cautious. He wouldn't release the crime scene until he'd had every blood drop checked a couple of times and every inch of ground examined with a magnifying glass.

On the other side of the valley, the Glyder range soared up

to the majestic Tryfan and provided some of the best climbing in the area—but it was a good two-hour hike away. It probably wasn't worth taking his climbing gear up there so late in the day, but at least a hike would blow away the cobwebs and maybe help him to think things through. Nothing made sense about the murders of last week, and yet nagging at the back of his mind was a feeling that he had overlooked something important. If he could only find the connection between the murders, he'd have them solved.

He changed into cordoroys and a T-shirt, stuffed his rain jacket into a knapsack, and tried to creep out before Mrs. Williams could snare him for lunch. He caught a glimpse of the table already laid, groaning under ham and tongue, a slab of cheese, salads, and cakes—everything cold, of course, because it was Sunday, and Mrs. Williams was one of the older generation who still did no work on the Sabbath.

"You're not going out, are you, Mr. Evans?" a voice called from the kitchen as Evan tried to open the front door silently. "I've got my daughter coming over later, and Sharon will be with her. They're looking forward to seeing you again."

"I've got some things that need doing, Mrs. Williams," Evan said as she appeared in the hall, not wearing her apron because it was Sunday.

"But you will be back later, won't you?" she asked. "Sharon would be so disappointed if she didn't see you and I've got a lovely lunch all ready . . ." Her voice trailed off hopefully.

Evan tried to think of a brilliant excuse for being absent until midnight, but couldn't. "I expect I'll be back later," he said.

He left the village without meeting anyone else and crossed a couple of rough pastures, scattering sheep as he went. The narrow sheep track started to climb up Glyder Fawr, the larger of the twin peaks. Evan scrambled up, jumping from rock to rock until Llanfair lay below like a toy village. Down the Nant-gwynant Pass there were tantalizing glimpses of blue ocean, and he could smell the fresh tang on the breeze. He took deep breaths and felt the tension slip away.

His gaze swept in a semicircle, taking in the toy cars creeping up the pass, the Sunday coaches belching out diesel fumes as they paused for photo ops and the slopes of Snowdon itself, Yr Wyddfa, deserted for once except for the sheep. Then he looked into a little hollow on the mountain ahead of him and he saw her. What he saw made his heart skip a beat.

Bronwen was kneeling there among the tall grass and spring flowers, lost in contemplation. Her long blond hair was blowing out free behind her and her pale blue skirt was spread in a circle around her so that she looked like a creature of legend—a water sprite who lured mortals to their death, maybe. This time he made sure that he didn't startle her.

"Hey, Bronwen," he called, when he was still far off.

She looked up and he saw that her eyes were shining. "Look," she said. "I've found one."

Her hands were cupped around a small white, tuliplike flower. "A Snowdon lily," she said. "I didn't know there were any up here! I must call the Nature Conservancy to put a wire fence around it so that the sheep don't eat it."

Evan was reminded sharply of his boyhood. He remembered climbing with his grandfather to look for the first Snowdon lilies and his grandfather's delight at finding one. In those days it wasn't that unusual to see them. Now it was very rare, even though they were a protected species. It was nice to know there were people like Bronwen around who still cared. He took the last few strides and sat on a rock beside her.

"Any news on Dilys yet?" she asked, looking up at him hopefully. "I couldn't stand it any more down there. I had to get away."

"We've found her," Evan said. "She's okay. She was running away to her auntie's house because she got in trouble at home."

Bronwen let out a sign of relief. "See, I knew it would be something simple. People always underestimate how sensitive teenagers are. They make fun or they tease or they scold and they think it's no big deal, but to a teenager it's life or death."

Evan nodded. "Dilys ran away because she caught her sister reading her diary. She gave her a good wop, apparently, and got yelled at for hitting her sister," he said. "Her sister wasn't punished. Dilys thought that wasn't fair."

Bronwen shook her head. "I don't suppose there was anything incriminating in the diary to begin with," she said, "but she's safely back now and that's all that matters. For a moment last night . . ." She looked away, staring out down the pass." I was really afraid."

"Yes, me too," Evan admitted. "I really want to congratulate you on the way you handled everything, Bron. You were so good with the Thomases. I was glad to have you there."

Bronwen shrugged but she looked pleased. "You get used to handling parents in my profession," she said. "Pity the dance ended early. I was looking forward to watching you do the tango with Betsy."

"Give over, Bronwen," Evan said with an embarrassed grimace. "I don't encourage her, you know. She just gets these ideas and . . ."

"It's okay. You don't owe me any explanations," Bronwen said, smiling. "What are you doing up here? You didn't come to keep an eye on me, did you?"

198

"I didn't know you were up here until now," Evan said. "I just needed to stretch my legs and try to make sense of these murders."

"They're no nearer to solving them then?"

Evan shook his head. "We might have ruled out a couple of possible suspects, but we don't know if we're dealing with one killer or two, and we've no idea of a motive." He got to his feet. "Look, I'm disturbing you. You probably don't want to hear me babbling on about my problems."

She reached out and touched his knee. "Don't go," she said. "I've done what I came up here to do. I've got all the time in the world if you want to talk."

Evan gave her a grateful smile and sat again. Bronwen swivelled around to face him, hugging her knees to her. "So tell me what you have to go on so far."

"Not much," Evan said. "We know the two men who fell to their deaths last Sunday—a week ago today, wasn't it?—were friends from their army days. We know they were invited by somebody to meet on the mountain on the anniversary of a fourth friend's death. Danny Bartholemew, a local boy from Portmadog. He died during army survival training on the mountain six years ago."

"Do you know who sent the invitation?"

Evan shook his head. "No idea. The one surviving friend, who chose not to go to the reunion, thought it was Tommy Hatcher, because it had a London postmark."

"But it wasn't?"

"He was one of the ones who was killed. And his mother found a similar postcard among his things."

"Why wait all this time to hold a memorial?" Bronwen asked.

"Precisely," Evan said. "It seems kind of ghoulish to me. I

199

would have thought that their friend's death would be something that everyone would rather forget."

"Does he have relatives? A wife?" Bronwen asked.

"He has a mother—a terrible little woman with a huge chip on her shoulder."

"No father or brothers?"

Evan shook his head. "All dead. She blames the English for taking all her men from her and leaving her alone."

"Oh, one of those," Bronwen said. "I was just thinking that the only reason to lure those men up onto the mountain might be revenge. What if someone close to Danny thought that his friends had let him down somehow and wanted to punish them. He or she lured them here on the pretext of a memorial service and then pushed them over, one by one."

Evan frowned. "It's possible."

"What other motive could there be?" She looked up at him. "You don't believe that's what happened then?"

"First of all, it wasn't anyone's fault that Danny died. The soldiers were sent off alone, at intervals, so nobody could be accused of abandoning him. And somehow he lost his pack with his survival gear in it."

"Maybe the person who cared about Danny doesn't see it that way. Maybe he had a sweetheart who has been brooding about it all these years. Maybe there was another soldier buddy we don't know about. Maybe even his mother . . ."

"She'd never be strong enough to push those men over a cliff," Evan said. "They were big men, you know, and fit too."

"She could have hired somebody."

"A hit man, you mean?"

"She could have got hold of a rabid Welsh nationalist and convinced him that he'd be striking a blow against the English if he avenged Danny's death."

Evan chuckled.

"I don't see what's so funny," Bronwen said, sounding hurt.

"I'm sorry," Evan said, "but I just can't see that happening. I think you only see revenge as a motive in Shakespeare's plays. I don't think people go around killing for revenge much in the real world."

"You don't?"

Evan shook his head. "No, I'd say revenge is a pretty poor motive for killing someone. In my experience most murders are for the basest of reasons—fear or greed or lust. Anyone who kills another human being is down at the level of the animals, and animals don't kill for revenge."

"An eye for an eye, a tooth for a tooth?" Bronwen suggested.

"I know a bit about revenge myself," Evan said. "I thought about it a lot when my dad was killed."

"Your father was killed? When?"

"Not too long ago."

"Evan, how terrible. You said he was a policeman too, didn't you? What happened?"

"He was trying to intercept a drug shipment, down on the docks. They shot wildly as they ran away. It only took one bullet, right through the heart." He stopped and took a deep breath. Even now it hurt physically to talk about it. "Right afterwards I was angry enough to have killed. If I'd caught the man who did it right away, I could have strangled him with my bare hands. But anger cools down. When they did catch them, they were little more than kids. They'd shot wildly because they were scared. What good would it do to take another life because one was lost so stupidly?"

"Is that why you came up here to Llanfair?" Bronwen asked.

Evan stared out across the valley. "I couldn't take it down there any more. I wanted to be somewhere that made sense."

"I understand perfectly," Bronwen said gently.

"But you can't run away from the world, can you? Here I am in the quietest, most peaceful corner of Wales, and the murders here are just as brutal and just as terrible as they were down in Swansea."

"No, you can't run away," Bronwen agreed. "I suppose humans are pretty much the same wherever you find them." She broke off a tall blade of grass and chewed on it. "So do you have any suspects at all so far?"

Evan shook his head. "Not really. Stewart Potts had a wife who was actually seen in Llanberis and wasn't too happily married to him. She says she came up here to check on him, because she thought he was meeting another woman. I suppose she could have shoved him off a cliff, but why kill anyone else? And it looks like she's a damn sight worse off without him.

"And then there's the fourth friend, the one who didn't come to the reunion. He wasn't where he claimed to be last Sunday, but his excuse made sense to me, and he has a cast-iron alibi for the other murder on Friday."

"You still think the same person was responsible for all three killings?"

"I don't know," Evans said. "On the face of it, I'd say no. Two were sneaky murders. Creeping up behind someone and pushing them off a cliff is a cowardly thing to do, isn't it. Cutting a throat is a violent, desperate act, or even an act of retaliation. It could be that we're looking for two separate murderers, Bron."

"What about Daft Dai?" Bronwen asked. "Might he be telling the truth that he committed the first two murders?"

"He might," Evan said.

"And what if the other killer is the same man who killed that little girl?"

Evan shrugged. "I don't know. I'm not an expert in psychology. They say that child molesters are usually meek and mild people most of the time, but if he was hiding out in the mountains and someone recognized him, he might be desperate enough to wait around and sneak up behind . . ." He paused, his mouth open. "Wait a second, Bron. We never looked into that angle, did we? We never checked whether this Lou Walters, the child molester, was in the army with the others. I'll look into that tomorrow."

Bronwen got to her feet. "This grass is damp," she said, brushing off her skirt, "and I should be getting back down. I've got papers to correct before class tomorrow. At least you've got another angle to look into now, haven't you?"

"Right," Evan said, standing up too and trying not to lose his train of thought as she shook out that luxuriant hair. "Who knows, maybe I've been going in the wrong direction all the time up to now. I felt all along that this must have something to do with the army but the other poor kid, Simon Herries, has no army connections at all. And I even had my suspicions about the major. You know, Major Anderson from the inn? I thought he might have been one of the officers who got demoted as a result of the inquiry into Danny's death."

"But you've proved he wasn't?"

Evan grinned. "It turns out he wasn't even in the army; he's one of those types who just goes around calling himself major."

"How about that," Bronwen said, smiling too.

"Pity really," Evan said. "He was in the right place at the right time to be a suspect too. Sergeant Watkins is checking into his background, but I can't see what possible motive he could have. He moves in very different circles from those two former army privates. I wouldn't have minded finding him guilty."

Bronwen wagged a finger. "You mustn't let personal animosities enter into a professional investigation," she said.

"I know," Evan said. "I don't even know why I'm getting involved in this. Detective Inspector Hughes has taken over the case himself, and I'm not even a part of his criminal investigation department. I'm supposed to confine my activities to finding lost cats and missing tourists." He glanced down at the bulky Victorian silhouette of the Powell-Jones house. At least Mrs. Powell-Jones was now satisfied.

Bronwen touched his arm lightly. "I think you're doing very well, Evan," she said. "I think you make a great policeman."

As she stood there on a rock the breeze sprang up and swept her hair and skirts out behind her, so that again she looked like a maiden from distant legend. Evan stood staring at her. He hadn't fully realized before how lovely she was.

"What are you looking at?" she asked sharply.

"You," Evan said. "You look really beautiful today, Bronwen, so sort of . . . magical and . . . unspoiled," he finished, searching for words that wouldn't come. He couldn't find the right word in Welsh either.

"There's something you should know about me," she said. "I came to Llanfair straight from a failed marriage. I've needed time to heal, just like you."

With that she started down the track ahead of him, her hair flying out behind her like spun gold.

Chapter 20

It was cold on the mountain that night. The wind moaned through the rocks and it was impossible to keep warm. Were they ever going to lift that damned police cordon? He couldn't risk coming down until he knew that the police weren't watching. Surely they'd found everything they were going to find. They'd been over the place with their absurd tweezers and plastic bags and metal detectors and they had been completely blind to what must have been staring them in the face. But it was okay. He could afford to wait, like a spider patiently beside its web. Sooner or later a fly would come.

On Monday morning Evan drove down to police HQ in Caernarfon and sought out Sergeant Watkins.

"Listen, sarge," he blurted out before Watkins could say anything. "I've got another idea worth checking on. Did anyone ever check whether Lou Walters was in the army?"

"What's this about the army?" a sharp voice asked behind them. D.I. Hughes was standing there, a dapperly dressed little man with perfectly styled graying hair and just a hint of a moustache.

"He was wondering if Lou Walters had been in the army," Sergeant Watkins said.

"What for?" D.I. Hughes was looking at Evan with cold blue eyes.

"If he had been, then the murders might be somehow tied together," Evan said.

D.I. Hughes seemed to focus on Evan for the first time. "Who are you exactly?" he asked. "I don't recall seeing you."

"Let me introduce P.C. Evans, sir," Sergeant Watkins said for him. "From Llanfair. He was the one who discovered the bodies and alerted us to possible foul play in the first deaths. He's an expert on mountain climbing."

"Is he now?" D.I. Hughes couldn't have sounded less interested. "And on the army?"

"It was just a thought, sir," Evan said. "Seeing that we've now found out the two men who fell to their deaths were in the army together and they came here for a memorial to another soldier who had died."

"What's this?" D.I. Hughes asked. Evan noticed too late Watkins shaking his head behind the D.I.'s back.

"We've been looking into various possible connections between the men and the death of a soldier on the mountain six years ago," Sergeant Watkins said. "We wanted to wait until all the facts were in before we presented them to you."

"We?" D.I. Hughes asked. "Have you been assigned to this department, Evans?"

"No, sir. I just wanted to help out," Evan said.

"I'm sure we're very grateful for all your help," D.I. Hughes said. "But I suggest you get back to your assigned duties and leave the criminal investigation to those trained to do it. And that's an order."

"Yes sir," Evan said. He glanced at Watkins but Watkins was busy studying a list on his desk and their eyes didn't meet.

As Evan went out he heard D.I. Hughes' crisp, clear voice. "Why didn't you tell him to get lost, Watkins? An untrained amateur is the last thing we need around here. Who knows how many potential witnesses he's scared off with his bumbling interrogations?"

"Oh, no. Evans is a good man, sir," Watkins replied. "We only discovered the army connection because of him."

"In future, Watkins, you will follow my line of investigation, not go rushing off in all directions on your own, is that clear?"

"Yes, sir," Watkins mumbled.

Evan didn't wait around any longer. He headed back down the hallway. He had now been officially ordered to stay off the case, but they couldn't stop him from satisfying his own curiosity, could they? He decided to take a peek at those old newspapers again. Maybe there was something he had overlooked in the reports on Danny Bartholemew's death—a name, perhaps, that had meant nothing then, or even a photo of someone he might now recognize.

He brought the relevant issue of the newspaper up onto the screen. The banner headline flashed out at him. MAIL TRAIN ROBBERY, and beneath it was a map. Evan's eyes took in the details of the map before he moved on to the next page. Then, on impulse, he went back again. He remembered the train thundering past when he was at the roadside cafe with Watkins. It was not too far from there that the robbery had taken place, and the trucks carrying the soldiers from Yorkshire would have driven along that very road . . . was it just co-incidence that the robbery and the exercises took place on the same day? He couldn't see what possible connection a train robbery and Danny Bartholemew's death could have had, but it was worth looking into.

This time he read the lead article in detail, then followed the story through subsequent days. In the end he was not much wiser, but he had picked up the name of the detective from Scotland Yard who was in charge of the case. It might be worth calling him when he got home.

Sitting alone in the tiny Llanfair police station, Evan had second thoughts about what he was going to do. Going behind a D.I.'s back and calling direct to Scotland Yard, especially when the D.I. had told him to mind his own business, could result in pretty serious punishment. Could he be dismissed for it, he wondered? It all depended how much clout D.I. Hughes had and how much his own chief was prepared to take his side. Of course, if he managed to solve the cases . . . Nobody could be fired for bringing a murderer to justice, could they?

He picked up the phone and dialed. He had a little speech thought out and was ready to argue his way through the min-ions to D.C.I. Harmon at Scotland Yard. He was surprised when the phone was picked up and a voice at the other end barked, "Harmon."

"Sir, this is Evans from North Wales police," Evan stam-mered, caught off guard. "We're looking into a couple of mur-ders up here that could possibly have something to do with the mail train robbery of six years ago. I understand you were the lead detective on that case. If you have a moment, I'd appre-ciate it if you could fill me in on some details."

"I never have a moment," Harmon said dryly. "I'm always

supposed to be somewhere ten minutes ago, but I'll answer a couple of questions if I can. Not that we like being reminded of that case, here at the Yard. It was one of our more spectacular failures." He paused for a second. "What do you need to know?"

Evan cleared his throat. "I'm not even sure of that myself, sir," he said. "I was just wondering if it was complete coincidence that a truckload of soldiers must have passed close to the site of the mail train robbery and that one of those soldiers died that same night." He stopped talking, aware that even to him it sounded ridiculous. He expected the chief inspector to bark at him for wasting his time.

"So what exactly are you asking me?" Harmon demanded.

"Is it possible that there was any sort of army connection?" Evan asked.

"Army connection? In what way?"

"That any of the robbers had something to do with the army?"

"Hardly," Harmon said with a dry laugh. "These boys hadn't done a day's work in their lives."

"Do you know who they all were?"

"Oh, yes. We know who they were all right. Not that we can do much about it. They called themselves the Bank Street Gang after some train robbery they'd seen in an old American movie, I think. Actually they were a conglomeration of several big-time thieves who usually worked the greater London area. They had it all planned down to the last detail, I'll give them that. The moment the money was off that train, they all split up into different directions, presumably each with some of the loot. They had small planes waiting at God knows how many private airfields, and they were in France or Ireland before we could warn anyone. The ones we caught were only small fry.

They had no money on them and they weren't talking either. It was hard to pin the robbery on them, especially since we knew their bosses got away without a scratch." He paused for breath. "Does this help at all?"

"Not really," Evan said.

"Look—we've got a whole bloody filing cabinet fill of stuff relating to this case. You're welcome to come down and take a look at it, if you think there might be something. But army connection? No, I can't see that. In fact, I think I can safely say that they'd be very antiarmy. McMahon and Connor, two of the leaders, were both Irish—and strongly anti-English in their sympathies. We even suspect some of the money went to the IRA."

"And they're both in South America now?"

"As far as we know," Harmon said. "Of course they're on fake passports, so it's hard to prove, but we've had eyewitness sightings. Nothing we can do about it, of course. It almost makes me feel bad that the poor sods we caught are doing ten to fifteen behind bars and got nothing out of it. Still, petty criminals were never known for their great brains, were they?"

"How many did you actually manage to catch?" Evan asked, more for a reason to keep the conversation going than because he wanted to know.

"Let's see. Four, I think. Five if you count Bartholemew."

"Bartholemew?" Evan almost shouted. "Danny Bartholemew was involved in this?"

"No, the name wasn't Danny," Harmon said. "Doug. That's right. Douglas Bartholemew. He was stopped for speeding on the outskirts of Birmingham and luckily his nervous behavior made them check on his record. He had a string of outstanding warrants as long as my arm. So luckily we didn't need the train robbery to put him away, although we know he'd worked with Connor and McMahon in the past—just as a hanger-on, mark you. Small fry. Not one of the big boys."

Evan's heart was racing. "Did this Doug Bartholemew come from Wales, do you know?"

"Possibly. Yes, now I come to think of it, he spoke with some kind of funny accent—no offence meant, of course."

"And where is he now?" Evan asked excitedly.

"I told you. He had enough outstanding warrants to put him away without having to try and implicate him in the mail train business. He's doing ten to fifteen in Pentonville."

"Oh," Evan said, his face falling again. It had all seemed so hopeful. Mrs. Bartholemew had complained that the English had taken both her sons from her and Evan had assumed that meant they were both dead. But she had meant that one was in jail. Unfortunately a jail cell was about the most perfect alibi anyone could have—which was a pity, because Doug Bartholemew could well have been eaten up with thoughts of revenge.

"Well, thanks for your help, sir," Evan said.

"Was I any help?" Harmon asked.

"You've cleared one thing up," Evan said, "but it doesn't leave us any further along, unfortunately."

"As I say, come on down if you want to go through the files," Harmon said. "There might be something else that may help."

"Thanks, sir," Evan said. "Thanks for your time."

"Not at all. We coppers have to help each other, don't we?"

Evan nodded to himself as he put down the phone. A nice chap. No wonder he'd gone to the top. He was the sort that his men would willingly put in overtime for. Not like that cold fish Hughes.

He got up and paced around the room. At least he was

right in one thing. He had sensed there was a connection between Danny and the mail train robbery and there was. But he didn't see how it could have helped. Doug was picked up in Birmingham right after the robbery. That was going fast in the wrong direction for Wales. And he was in custody when Danny reached Wales and subsequently froze to death on the mountain. And he was still in custody, doing ten to fifteen.

Evan reached for his jacket and went out. It was one of those too bright days that can't be trusted in Wales. The wind was rustling through the oak trees behind the police station and whipping at the grass. With that strength of westerly, the weather could change in a hurry. But right now it was good walking weather. Evan strode out up the village street. He nodded to Evans-the-Post who was just coming out of the post office with his laden bag over his shoulder.

"Any juicy ones today?" Evan called out to him.

"I haven't had a chance to see yet," Evans-the-post called back. "She won't let me look at them." He indicated the post office where Miss Roberts treated him, and her customers, like naughty schoolchildren.

Evan walked on, past the pub. The Red Dragon sign squeaked in the wind. It was about time somebody oiled that hinge, he thought and found himself picturing Betsy climbing up there in her too short skirt. Keep your mind on the job, he told himself severely. Somehow all this patchwork of events had to be linked together, had to make sense. He remembered Betsy saying in surprise," Funny old place to hold a reunion." She hadn't been wrong. It was a funny old place. Someone wanted those men up on the mountain for a reason. Was that reason to kill them? And if someone wanted them dead, why not make it simpler? There were many ways to kill a person in

London or in Liverpool, without bringing them all the way to Wales.

Evan continued up the street. It was recess at the school and the children were making a racket as they ran around, squealing and yelling. Evan paused to watch. Young children always amazed and impressed him. They lived every moment to the full with their unself-conscious noise and uninhibited actions. They didn't stop to worry whether they looked foolish or what anyone would think. That didn't come until they got older—like poor Dilys, who hated to be teased and kept all her thoughts in a very secret diary and got punished because she lost her temper when her sister snooped.

He could hear Dilys' clear young voice saying, "She poked her nose where it had no business to be."

An alarm bell was buzzing at the back of Evan's brain. What if that third killing, the one of the young Oxford student that didn't make sense, had been because he was in the wrong place at the wrong time, like Dilys' sister?

Okay, Evan said to himself, building on this. Why was it the wrong place? Because someone was hiding up there, maybe? Because he stumbled on someone in the act of doing something illegal or wrong? He thought of Lou Walters, the child molester again. They should have caught him by now but he had eluded them so far. What if he was hiding out up there? What if Simon Herries had caught him hiding a child's body, or killing a missing child? Then he'd have to be killed to shut him up, wouldn't he?

Finally something was beginning to make sense. Maybe the killings were unrelated after all and maybe Lou Walters was still hiding out on the mountain, scared to move because there was still a police presence up there and the ways down were being watched!

Evan picked up the pace. He'd go and look for himself right away. He'd been so anxious to tie these crimes to a tragedy that happened six years ago that he'd overlooked the glaring fact that a suspected murderer was on the loose. He didn't know what he'd find up at the crime scene, but he was hopeful of finding something that Hughes and his team had overlooked.

He drew level with the chapels and was deep in thought when a voice yelled, "Yoo hoo! Constable Evans. Over here!"

Evan looked up to see Mrs. Powell-Jones beckoning violently from her garden. "Get over here, man. There's more evidence," she yelled.

Reluctantly Evan came across to her.

"What do you make of this then?" she demanded. "I raked that bed yesterday."

She pointed at a bed of bare earth that ran along the back of her garden, beside the back hedge. In the middle of that bed there was now one large footprint.

"It looks like you got the wrong man, constable," she said triumphantly. "I imagine that your mentally challenged suspect is still locked in a cell, but someone continues to trample on my vegetable beds."

Evan stared at the footprint and shrugged. "I don't know why anyone would come into your garden to walk over your flower beds, Mrs. Powell-Jones," he said. He looked up. The yew hedge was not equally thick all the way along and through it Evan had a good view of the Everest Inn and the yellow police tape across the path beyond it. It suddenly occurred to him that this would be a great vantage point for anybody to watch both the inn and the path up Snowdon. He couldn't think why anybody would want to watch the inn or the path, but he couldn't think of any other reason for wanting to trample Mrs. Powell-Jones' beds.

"Look, Mrs. Powell-Jones, I've got something I have to check into up on the mountain," he said, "but I'll give this my full attention when I come back down."

"Please hurry up then," she called after him as he forced his way through the hedge and out to the meadow beyond. "I've got runner beans waiting to be planted and I'm not putting them in until someone can guarantee that no large feet will be trampling them. We do pay our taxes you know. We expect protection from our police force."

Evan wondered about Mrs. Powell-Jones' logic—she seriously thought that catching a vandal who walked on her flower beds was more important than catching a murderer. Evan supposed she was like a lot of people—convinced her own problems were more important than anyone else's. He put Mrs. Powell-Jones from his mind and forced his legs into overdrive in an effort to get up the mountain as quickly as possible.

He took the Pig Track, the steeper of the two routes, because it was also faster. By the time he had ascended above Llyn Llydaw, he was gasping for breath and realized that he hadn't stopped to eat all day. He was glad that nobody could see him leaning against a rock, panting. Very bad for his image, he thought. He was lucky that the mountain was still off-limits and he wasn't likely to bump into anyone he knew.

Then he stiffened and instinctively shrunk behind the outcrop. A figure had just left the Everest Inn and was hurrying up the track, past the yellow police tape. As he came out of the shadow of a little stand of larch trees, Evan recognized him. It was Major Anderson.

215

Chapter 21

Evan didn't waste another second. He couldn't guess what reason the major could have for coming up the trail behind him, but he had to assume the worst—that he was being followed. And indeed, when he glanced back again, he saw that Major Anderson was moving carefully, trying to blend in with the shadows of the rocks.

Evan was half tempted to go back down and confront him, but more urgently he had to get up to the place where Simon Herries was murdered and find out why it had been a fatal mistake for Simon to have sheltered there.

His heart was hammering from the exertion as he took the rocky steps up the mountain in giant strides. When he drew level with Glaslyn, the little upper lake, he skirted carefully around the edge and then scrambled up the sheet of scree and loose rocks to the cave where Simon's body had been found. There was still another ring of yellow police tape around it, but no policemen were in sight. The light clouds had thickened into a heavy, gray layer, only occasionally broken by patches of blue that let shafts of sunlight down onto the rocks. A shaft hit the rocks above Evan as he scrambled up carefully, not wanting to set off a slide of the unstable scree. For a moment it lit up the entrance to the cave, like the hand of God from an old Romantic painting. Evan found the hair at the back of his neck prickling.

He didn't know what had made him come up here and only now realized that it might have been a very foolish move, as well as a defiant one. Until now his only concern had been possible trouble with his superiors. Now it occurred to him that he might be risking more than an unpleasant session in his chief's office. Cloud had already blotted out the summit above him. He had never felt alone in the high country before, but now he felt completely cut off from the world below, beyond help if it was needed.

But he couldn't turn back now. He was sure that something that held the key to three murders had been overlooked in that cave and he had to find it now, or never. He reached the mouth of the little cave and eased his way past the slab of fallen rock across its door. The smell of death still lingered. The floor had now been swept smooth, and presumably every fragment was currently being analyzed by the lab, but it was impossible to clean the bloodstains off the rock. They lay in spatters and trickles, like a modern painting.

Why? Evan asked himself. Why was he killed here?

As he examined the back of the cave, he saw that his initial theory was wrong. Simon Herries couldn't have surprised someone hiding out in the cave. It was impossible for anyone to have been hiding behind the rock where Simon had rested. True it had been a former mine entrance once, but the ceiling had come down and filled the passageway with large rocks. Whoever cut Simon's throat must have come up behind him and taken him by surprise, so Simon would have had to be facing into the cave, maybe checking out what had once been a passageway into the mine. Evan squeezed past the boulder where they had found his body and tried to see how extensive the collapse had been. Was there still a passageway behind it? Was it possible to get through if he tried to move some of the rocks out of the way?

He cursed himself for not bringing a flashlight. He tried lifting the first few rocks aside. Most of them were too big for one man to handle alone and Evan soon stopped, not sure of the point of the exercise any longer. If he couldn't move the rocks to get through, then nobody else could either. A waste of time and effort.

You don't really know what you're doing, do you? He chided himself. You're just playing at detective.

Then he glimpsed it at his feet—just a fraction of what looked like a belt or a strap sticking out from under the rock pile. He tried to get to his knees in that narrow space and to move the rocks so that he could see what he was looking at. He had to hold his breath and squeeze down between rocks, but he could definitely see now that someone had been at work before him, trying to do the same thing. Loose rocks and earth had been scraped away. He tried pulling on the end of the strap, but whatever lay beyond was trapped by large rocks. He managed to dig out some more loose material until he had exposed the corner of something that felt like canvas. It was dark with mould, but there appeared to be markings on it. Evan managed to free his handkerchief and attempted to wipe it clean. The markings were letters, stencilled on. He could just make out 1BN, then a space and then something that started with Y.

1BN Y. Evan had seen those kind of stencilled letters before, and he could make a good guess at what they stood for. First Battalion, Yorkshire Regiment.

"Danny Bartholemew's pack," he said out loud.

"Nice work, copper," a voice said behind him and before he could stand up or turn around, he felt something hard jabbed into the small of his back. "Quite right," the voice went on. "Danny's pack. And you're going to help me get it out."

Evan turned his head slowly to look up at the owner of the voice. In the semidarkness he could make out a gaunt, hard-faced man, looking at him with expressionless eyes. Evan couldn't see the gun he was holding, but its barrel was already beginning to hurt as it dug into the soft flesh around his kidneys. He tried to match the face to the posters that had been circulated around HQ.

"You're not Lou Walters," he exclaimed.

The man looked surprised. "Lou who?" he said.

"Who are you then?" Evan demanded.

"Not very bright, are you?" the man said. He had a definite Welsh undertone to his voice, but it was now overlaid with the harsh cockney sounds of London. "But none of you coppers ever were too bright. I'm Danny's brother, Doug."

"Doug Bartholemew? But they said you were in jail—how did you manage to get out?"

Doug chuckled. "It's called the early release scheme, old son. There was shocking overcrowding so they let some of the good boys, like me, go home. Wasn't that kind of them?" His voice dripped with bitter sarcasm and Evan could sense that this was a person who cared nothing for human life. His only chance was to play along with whatever Doug Bartholemew wanted of him.

"Look, do you mind if I get out of this position," Evan said cautiously. "My knees are killing me." Instantly he regretted another poor choice of words. But the pressure of the gun barrel eased slightly.

"Go on then, stand up and back out but don't try any funny business," Dough said. "I'd kill you right now for two pins. I've got nothing to lose, but you're a big strong bloke and I need someone to move the rocks for me."

Cautiously Evan got to his feet. His legs felt strangly detached, although he couldn't tell if this was from fear or just pins and needles. As he stood up, the gun resumed its pressure with Doug right behind him. He knew he had to play for time.

"How long have you been out, Doug?" He asked as if he was chatting to someone in the pub.

"Almost a month," Doug said. "I came straight back home to my dear old mother."

Evan remembered the uneasiness he had felt when talking to Mrs. Bartholemew, the sense of being watched in her house. So Doug had been there all the time. If only he could have acted then . . .

"You were the one who sent the postcards and invited Danny's friends to the reunion," Evan said, gradually putting pieces together. "What were you trying to do, avenge Danny's death?"

"Avenge? Don't be so bloody stupid," Doug said. "My brother was a dumb kid and if he died, it was his own fault. No, old son, I'm more interested in two hundred thousand smackeroos I've got waiting for me under all those rocks."

Finally the last piece of the puzzle snapped into place in Evan's mind. "Danny had the money in his pack!" he said. "Your share of the train robbery money!"

"Very good," Douglas said with the same biting sarcasm. "It was a perfect plan, wasn't it? No way it could get screwed up. I drove away from the train with my share of the cash and dropped it off in some bushes behind a truck stop. All done in fifteen minutes. If they caught me after that, they'd have nothing to pin on me, would they?"

Except they did pin all those prior offenses on you, Evan thought, but wisely kept quiet. He had noted in the past that criminals tended to be cocky, also to underestimate the police.

"So you left the money," Evan prompted him.

"And Danny was due to pass by not too long afterwards. He got them to stop for him to take a leak, went back into the bushes behind the cafe, tipped out his stuff, and put the money in his pack. Then the plan was to leave the pack where it would be easy for me to pick up, and call me with the location. When the fuss had died down, I'd go up and get it. Perfect, eh? Only the stupid little bugger goes and twists his ankle and freezes to death up here in a freak snowstorm, and I get picked up for speeding."

"Bad luck," Evan said, hoping somehow to make some sort of connection with Doug.

"Bloody bad luck," Doug agreed. "And that's the stupid bloody English army for you too, isn't it? Leave a poor bloke to freeze up there? They're supposed to be looking after their own men, aren't they, not killing them off?"

"I don't quite understand what you hoped to get from this reunion," Evan said.

"Simple, isn't it?" Doug snorted. "I had no idea where Danny had hidden the money. I thought that maybe one of his mates could show me the route Danny had taken during those exercises. It was just possible he'd told one of them what he was going to do, even though I told him not to. So I hid out close to that inn place and then I followed the first bloke up the mountain. I thought I could get at least one of them to help me find Danny's pack. I was prepared to split it with him, but you know what happened, don't you? My bad luck again. The first bloke I spoke to turned out to be a fuckin' copper! He started asking a lot of questions and then he started getting suspicious. I'm not sure whether he recognized me, but I think he did. Anyway, I couldn't take the chance, could I? I got him to the right spot and when he wasn't looking, I shoved him over. Easy enough to do and everyone would think it was an accidental fall, wouldn't they?"

Not me, Evan thought, but again didn't say. "What about the other chap?" Evan asked.

"He saw, didn't he? I thought he'd already gone, but he hadn't. He looked back and saw me do it. I had to get around to him pretty damned quick. Lucky I know the mountain and he didn't. When he climbed out on that jutting rock to get a look at the first bloke's body, it was easy enough to sneak up behind him too. But I was no nearer to finding the stupid pack, was I?"

He adjusted his stance and the gun barrel dug sharply into Evan's side, making him wince. "So I started checking out the area, bit by bit. I didn't find this place right away, because of the slab of rock that's fallen across it. But when I finally found it, what good was it to me? I couldn't shift the bloody rocks by myself and the place was crawling with coppers. I thought it would be safe enough to wait. I didn't think anyone else would be likely to come snooping around, but that kid came in to shelter from the rain, and he found the pack too."

Evan looked back at him. His eyes were still expressionless.

"He was all excited as I came into the cave. He told me he'd found something buried under the rock fall. "Why don't we try and get it out together?" I suggested, but the little bugger said that no, he thought we should notify the authorities first. He was going to do that—tell the bloody park ranger!"

223

"So you killed him," Evan said flatly.

"Had to, didn't I?" Doug said. "I couldn't have him telling no park ranger!" He sucked through his teeth. "Of course, I realized later it was a bloody stupid thing to do. All those policemen snooping around. I was sure they were going to find it, even though I took care to pile up the rocks in front of it again. And I didn't think they were going to seal off the whole bloody mountain! I've had to hide out up here for three days now. I've hardly had a thing to eat in three days. There's nothing much in that bloody snack bar."

"You had an apple pie last week, didn't you?" Evan asked.

"Yeah. Not bad either," Doug said. "Why, was there a fuss about it?"

"A big fuss," Evan said.

Doug laughed. For a moment Evan hoped he was reaching him, that they were becoming mates, co-conspirators. This was dashed right away, when Doug went on laughing. "That's nothing compared to the fuss there will be when they find a dead copper up here."

"What makes you think I'll help you move the rocks if you're going to kill me anyway?" Evan asked.

"Experience," Doug said. "Most people want to stay alive as long as possible, don't they—on the off chance that something will turn up?"

"There are police all over this mountain, you know," Evan said. "You'd never get away with it."

"Nah," Doug said easily. "Yesterday that was true. Today the train hasn't come up once and they're all too bloody lazy to walk, I know that. So we're all alone, old son. Just you and me."

"Okay," Evan said. "Where do you want me to start?"

224

"It's obvious, ain't it?" Doug said. "Start lifting the rocks off the top until we get to the pack."

"And where do I put them?"

"Boy, I didn't think even coppers could be this thick," Doug sneered. "Drop them over there!"

He turned his eyes as Evan had hoped he would. Evan didn't hesitate. He dug his elbow hard into Doug's middle. He heard a hissed exhaling of breath as Doug doubled over, but he didn't lose control of the gun, as Evan had hoped. Grimacing in pain, he was already raising the gun to take aim as Evan darted out of the cave. The shot bounced off the rock just above Evan's head and echoed alarmingly. Chips of rock fell onto him as he ran. But the one wild shot had given him the second he needed. He was out of the cave.

Cloud now covered the summits above him. Like a wild thing, he scrambled up the last few yards on all fours, until he was swallowed up into the mist.

"You can't get away from me, copper." Doug's voice rang out behind him, and Evan heard rocks bouncing down as Doug scrambled up after him. Desperately Evan tried to decide what to do next. If the cloud just covered the summit, Doug could pick him off the moment he came out of it. That meant there was no safe way down to get help. His only chance was up. He knew these mountains better than almost anybody. He had to take the chance that he knew them better than Doug Bartholemew.

He kept scrambling blindly upward until he picked up a trail. Mist swirled about him, so thick that he could hardly see his feet. But he had to trust to his judgement that he had picked up the Miners' Track, right below the summit of Snowdon itself. And sure enough, a few more seconds of climbing and he saw the hard dark line of the train track, emerging from the mist. Doug would surely expect him to try to go down to Llanberis to get help. When the trail started to descend, following the railway, he ignored it, glancing down regretfully. Instead, he started to climb again.

"You're not getting away from me, copper," Doug's voice echoed.

In that blanket of mist it was hard to tell which direction sound was coming from. It echoed back from unseen rocks as if twenty Dougs were on the mountain. Then a shot whizzed past Evan's ear and he knew that Doug Bartholemew was right behind him. He surged onward and upward, dreading what lay before him as much as what was following. But he had no choice. If he had any hope of losing Doug Bartholemew, it would be on Crib Gogh. Only an insane person would try to cross that knife-edged crest in mist as thick as this, he decided. If he could cross it successfully, he'd have a chance of coming down the other side and dropping straight to the trees and the Everest Inn beyond.

The trail climbed in a series of uneven rocky steps. Mist had made the rocks wet, and his feet slithered as he went up, putting down his hands from time to time to steady himself. He heard a curse behind him as Doug also slipped and realized he might have underestimated his adversary. Doug was keeping up with him pretty well!

He sensed, rather than saw, that he had come onto Crib Goch. Through the shifting mist the trail went ahead, a thin rocky ribbon, slippery, uneven, and no wider than a stair runner. And on either side, nothing. He could feel the cold emptiness swirling up from below. One false step, one stagger, and it would be a thousand feet before he met the rocks. He heard pebbles bouncing down unseen rock faces and knew that Doug was still behind. He took a deep breath and ran.

It seemed to take forever. He felt himself trapped in a time warp, running in slow motion, one foot in front of the other, across a tightrope over an ocean of cloud. But his feet seemed to know the way. They moved forward with a life of their own, confident that this was just a repeat of something done often before, until at last he was conscious of land spreading out on either side of him and the trail going down.

He paused among the rocks to look back and listen. Total silence. There was no sound of Doug's boots nor of pebbles falling. Evan's skin prickled. He imagined Doug creeping up on him, the gun digging suddenly into his side.

Then a voice called through the mist, "Help me, copper. Come and get me."

Evan looked back. Clouds swirled, parted and then cleared for a moment. Doug Bartholemew was on all fours in the middle of Crib Goch, staring out with horror at the abyss that had opened up on either side of him.

"I can't move," he called. "Come and get me."

"Do you think I'm stupid?" Evan called. "Throw away the gun first!"

"I can't move," Bartholemew cried. "For God's sake come and get me off here!"

"Throw away the gun!" Evan yelled.

Inch by inch Doug Bartholemew moved his hand with the gun in it. Evan held his breath. Then his fingers opened and the gun went clattering down into the void.

"Now the knife!" Evan yelled, remembering Simon Herries.

"I don't have a knife!"

227

"The knife that killed Simon Herries!"

"I threw it away," Doug Bartholemew called back.

Still Evan hesitated. This was, after all, a man who had had the strength and cunning to hurl two men to their deaths—men as young and fit as Evan himself. Of course they were both caught off guard and Evan was prepared, but then they were not on Crib Goch. There was no margin for error. One quick shove, one second off balance, and he'd be over the edge. And yet there seemed to be genuine panic in the man's voice.

Bartholemew might have lost his nerve right now, Evan reasoned, but that wouldn't stop him from turning on his rescuer the moment he got a chance, and Evan didn't fancy a wrestling match so far from help. Why didn't the top brass let the ordinary policemen on the beat carry guns? A gun would have come in really handy right now. He peered down through the shifting clouds, still trying to make the right decision.

"Copper! For Christ's sake! Don't leave me here!" Doug Bartholemew shouted.

Evan stood like a statue, unable to make up his mind between prudence and valour. He could imagine Inspector Hughes' face if he brought in the murderer, single-handed. Then he found himself thinking of his father. Had his father dreamed of being a hero too when he went alone to intercept that drug shipment in the Swansea docks? Better to play it safe, Evan decided. Doug was in no danger as long as he didn't try to move. Wouldn't it be sensible to leave him there while he went for help? It would do him good to let him feel the terror his victims felt.

"Hang on, Doug, I'm going for help," he called back. "I won't be long."

He took two steps down the track and stopped short.

Major Anderson was standing there, blocking the path ahead and watching him.

"What's going on, constable?" he asked. He was smiling pleasantly and he sounded friendly enough but Evan caught an edge of suppressed excitement in his voice.

Play it cool, Evan told himself. There's no way you can take on two of them.

"Oh, major, am I glad to see you," he said. "There's a man stuck on Crib Goch. I was about to go and get help to bring him down. Maybe you'd like to do it for me?"

Major Anderson pushed past Evan and stared through the shifting clouds. "No need to do that," he said. "Surely we can get him safely down between us?"

"He might panic and be hard to control," Evan said. "I've known people do that."

"I think I can handle panic," Major Anderson said. "You out there," he called to Doug Bartholemew, "we're coming to get you. Don't move until we tell you to."

Evan's heart was thumping so loudly he was sure that the major must be able to hear it. He couldn't see how the major fitted in, but what was he doing up here if he had nothing to do with the crime?

Major Anderson had already begun to walk out onto the knife edge. Evan realized he might be walking into a trap, and yet he couldn't just stand there and watch the major trying to rescue Doug alone either. It had become a matter of honor. Maybe his father had felt the same way when he recognized the drug dealers and knew he had to go on anyway . . .

He took a deep breath and walked out onto Crib Goch.

"Just a minute, major," he said. "Before we get to him, I should warn you that he's the murderer we've been looking for. This whole thing could be a trap."

"Does he have a weapon?"

"He threw his gun away. He says he doesn't have a knife."

"You take his left arm, I'll grab his right," Major Anderson said in a low voice. "We'll lift him to his feet and drag him off when I say go."

Evan nodded.

Until now Evan had felt as if he was part of a cartoon world, a Looney Tune character being chased up and down mountains. Now time froze. It took an eternity to reach down and take Doug's left arm. He saw the major, his mirror image, on the other side of Doug.

"Up you get, my man," Major Anderson said briskly. He took Doug's arm and bent it behind his back. "Any funny business and I'll snap this like a matchstick," he added.

"Don't hurt me. I'll do what you say," Doug whined. He was as limp as a rag doll as they dragged him to his feet and half carried him to safety.

"There you are. Piece of cake," Major Anderson said, grinning at Evan as they stood gasping among the rocks beyond Crib Goch.

Evan struggled to remove his tie. "Keep hold of him for a moment, major," he said as Doug grimaced at the major's grip on his arm.

Swiftly Evan bound his tie around the man's wrists. "Douglas Bartholemew, I arrest you for the murders of Tommy Hatcher, Stewart Potts, and Simon Herries," he said. "You have the right to remain silent. Anything you say will be taken down and may be used against you in a court of law."

Chapter 22

"Good work, constable," Major Anderson said, shaking Evan's hand as the police car containing Doug Bartholemew drove off down the main street of Llanfair. "It was pretty damned brave of you to go up there alone."

"Pretty damned foolish, now that I think of it," Evan admitted.

"A man after my own heart," Major Anderson said.

"Thanks for your help, major," Evan said, the familiar flush of embarrassment creeping up his neck at this unexpected praise. "It was lucky you showed up. I might never have got him down safely alone. He's a crafty bugger. He might easily have turned on me once I'd rescued him. Just what were you doing up on the mountain anyway?" he demanded as an afterthought.

"Keeping an eye on you," Major Anderson said. "Your little schoolteacher friend came to me in great distress and said she'd seen you heading up the mountain and she didn't think it was safe for you to be up there alone. So I couldn't ignore a lady in distress, could I? I followed you. But you moved too damned fast for me and I lost you. You're too young and fit. Twenty years ago I was like that, of course. But that was when I was still in—"

"The army?" Evan asked innocently.

"The army? Good God no. Who told you I was in the army? I was a marine, my boy. Where they turn out real men!"

"The marines. How about that?" Evan said lamely. To hide his discomfort he turned away, letting his gaze wander across to the school yard. It was empty now. He wondered where Bronwen was and was impressed that she had been able to sense his danger and cared enough about him to have gone for help. Then his gaze moved on to the Victorian splendor of the Powell-Jones residence and an anticipatory smile spread across his face. "I should go and have a word with Mrs. Powell-Jones," he said.

"I think I should buy you a drink first." Major Anderson clapped a big hand on his shoulder. "You look like you could use one."

"Business before pleasure, major," Evan said. "But I wouldn't say no to a drink if you want to go ahead to the pub and order me one. I'll be with you in a couple of minutes."

"Fine. Excellent. Consider it done," Major Anderson said and strode off toward the swinging Red Dragon sign. Evan turned in the other direction and trudged up the hill to Mrs. Powell-Jones' house. His legs suddenly felt like lead. He hadn't realized until now how tired he felt, but an interview with Mrs. Powell-Jones could be just the tonic he needed to revive him.

Mrs. Powell-Jones opened the front door with a look of expectation. "I hope you've come to tell me you've finally found the real culprit, constable," she said. "And I shouldn't be surprised if it didn't turn out to be Mrs. Parry Davies after all, stomping around in big boots to put me off the scent. But I am not so easily fooled, constable, I—"

"Mrs. Powell-Jones," Evan said. "I think we should take a look in your garden shed."

"My garden shed?"

"Yes, how often do you go in there?"

"Me? Almost never. I keep my garden tools in the greenhouse now. That shed is far too damp."

"Ah," Evan said and strode forward to the shed at the bottom of the garden. It was very dark and damp inside, but there were clear signs of occupation, including an empty pie plate.

"Yours, I think," Evan said, handing it to Mrs. Powell-Jones.

"But I don't understand . . ." she began.

"Madam, you might be finding yourself in serious trouble," Evan said, eyeing her firmly. "Harboring a known criminal? Aiding and abetting—"

"What are you talking about?" Mrs. Powell-Jones demanded.

"Only that you had a murderer hiding out in your shed last week. I'm not sure whether you were privy to this or not. A known felon on your property . . . it won't look good. I hope the judge will be understanding."

"Are you trying to tell me that you suspect me?" She shrieked. "Me? A minister's wife? You think I might have been sheltering a criminal?"

"I'm just saying that we'll be looking into it further. Those allegations against Mrs. Parry Davies will all have to come out, of course. Libel is it, or slander? I always get those two mixed up . . ."

"But I never really suspected her," Mrs. Powell-Davies whispered. "I mean, why would she want to steal my apple pie? Her pastry is quite as good as mine. I won't be taken for interrogation, will I?"

"Don't worry, ma'am. I'll make sure they're gentle with you," Evan said. "I'll put in a good word for you if you like."

He gave her a half salute then left her staring at his back, her mouth open.

"The major's waiting for you in the lounge and he's ordered you a glass of brandy, Evan bach," Betsy called as Evan came into the public bar. "He said you'd caught the murderer single handed!" She beamed at him, her eyes glowing.

"The major helped too," Evan said. "It was just luck, you know."

"Don't you always be so modest, Evan Evans," Betsy said. "What you need is someone to blow your trumpet for you, if you're not willing to do it yourself. Sit you down now and get that brandy inside you."

Major Anderson hailed him from the table in the corner. "That little filly has got her eye on you, I think," he muttered as Evan sat.

Evan nodded.

"You could do worse. Good pair of—"

"Cheers, major, Iached da," Evan cut in quickly. He lifted the brandy glass and took a generous swig. "I'm not supposed to, on duty, but in this case I think it's warranted."

"Drinking on duty again? The D.I. won't like that, Evans!" Evan looked up to see Sergeant Watkins standing in the doorway. "I was in the squad car when the message came through," he said, "I was just on my way back from bringing in Lou Walters."

"Lou Walters? You caught him?"

"Yes, we followed his mother when she was taking food to

him. He was hiding in an abandoned warehouse. He came with us meek as a lamb. It was the mother who had to be subdued."

"Congratulations, sarge," Evan said.

"You too," Sergeant Watkins said. "I picked up the news on my radio and I came straight over to make sure you're all right."

"I'm fine, thanks, sarge. Much better now I've got this inside me." He indicated the glass.

"I must say that was bloody smart of you to figure out that the money from that train robbery was stashed away up there," Watkins went on. "It always comes down to something very basic in the end, doesn't it? Greed or fear or a bit of both." He grinned at Evan then looked down at the glass in his hand. "Is this a private party, or are you going offer something to your colleague who's driven all the way up from Bangor in a hurry?"

"I seem to remember that you should be doing the buying, sarge," Evan said. "What about our little bargain, eh?"

"I said I'd treat you to a pint if you found the murderer, didn't I? You're like a bloody elephant. You don't forget a thing," Watkins said, pulling up a chair beside Evan. "Anyway, beer and cognac don't mix. Grape and grain, you know. We'll have to save that beer for another day."

"I don't mind watching you put one away, sarge," Evan said. "What are you drinking?"

"I wouldn't say no to a Brains," Sergeant Watkins said.

"A South Wales beer, eh?" Evan joked. "I used to be a Brains drinker myself when I lived down there. But now I seem to have this taste for Guinness." He caught Betsy's eye. "Betsy, love, can you bring over a pint of Brains for my sergeant here?" he called.

"The name's Jack, by the way," Sergeant Watkins said, extending his hand to Evan.

"Evan," Evan said, shaking the offered hand.

"Evan Evans?" Watkins laughed. "You can't get more Welsh than that, can you?"

"Don't blame me. I got stuck with the stupid name. When I have kids I'm going to give them ordinary names so that they don't get teased," Evan said.

"Speaking of kids," Major Anderson muttered in a stage whisper. Evan followed his gaze to the doorway. Bronwen was standing there, her cheeks flushed, her hair windswept. She strode up to Evan and stood glaring down at him.

"Next time you want to do something bloody stupid like chasing murderers up mountains, you tell me about it first or you take me with you, Evan Evans," she said fiercely. Then she bent and kissed him full and hard on the mouth, before she stalked out again.

Evan leaped to his feet. "Bron, wait!" he called and ran out after her.

Charlie Hopkins, leaning against the public bar, looked at Betsy.

"Miss Milk and Water? Is that what you called her? I think you might have been wrong there, Betsy bach. In fact I reckon you've got quite a fight on your hands."

"We'll see about that, Charlie Hopkins," Betsy said defiantly, smoothing down her fuzzy black sweater. "We'll see about that, won't we?"

High above, the mountain rested.